SEASON of the CARNIVAL

3/24/84

Gunn —

Hope you enjoy my sideshows — Maybe it'll help you tolerate your own one day!

Ora Brokaw —

SEASON of the CARNIVAL

Ora Lindsay Graham

Thomas Nelson Publishers
Nashville • Camden • New York

My appreciation to
Evelyn Kistler Campbell
for her emotional support
and editorial assistance.

Copyright © 1984 by Ora Lindsay Graham

All rights reserved. Written permission must be secured from the publisher to use or reproduce any part of this book, except for brief quotations in critical reviews or articles.

Published in Nashville, Tennessee, by Thomas Nelson, Inc. and distributed in Canada by Lawson Falle, Ltd., Cambridge, Ontario.

Printed in the United States of America.

Library of Congress Cataloging in Publication Data

Graham, Ora Lindsay.
  Season of the carnival.

  1. Graham, Ora Lindsay. 2. Middle-aged women—United States—Biography. 3. Christian biography—United States. 4. Family—United States—Case studies.
I. Title.
HQ1059.5.U5G7 1984   305.4   83-25032
ISBN 0-8407-5888-X

In Memory of Mama

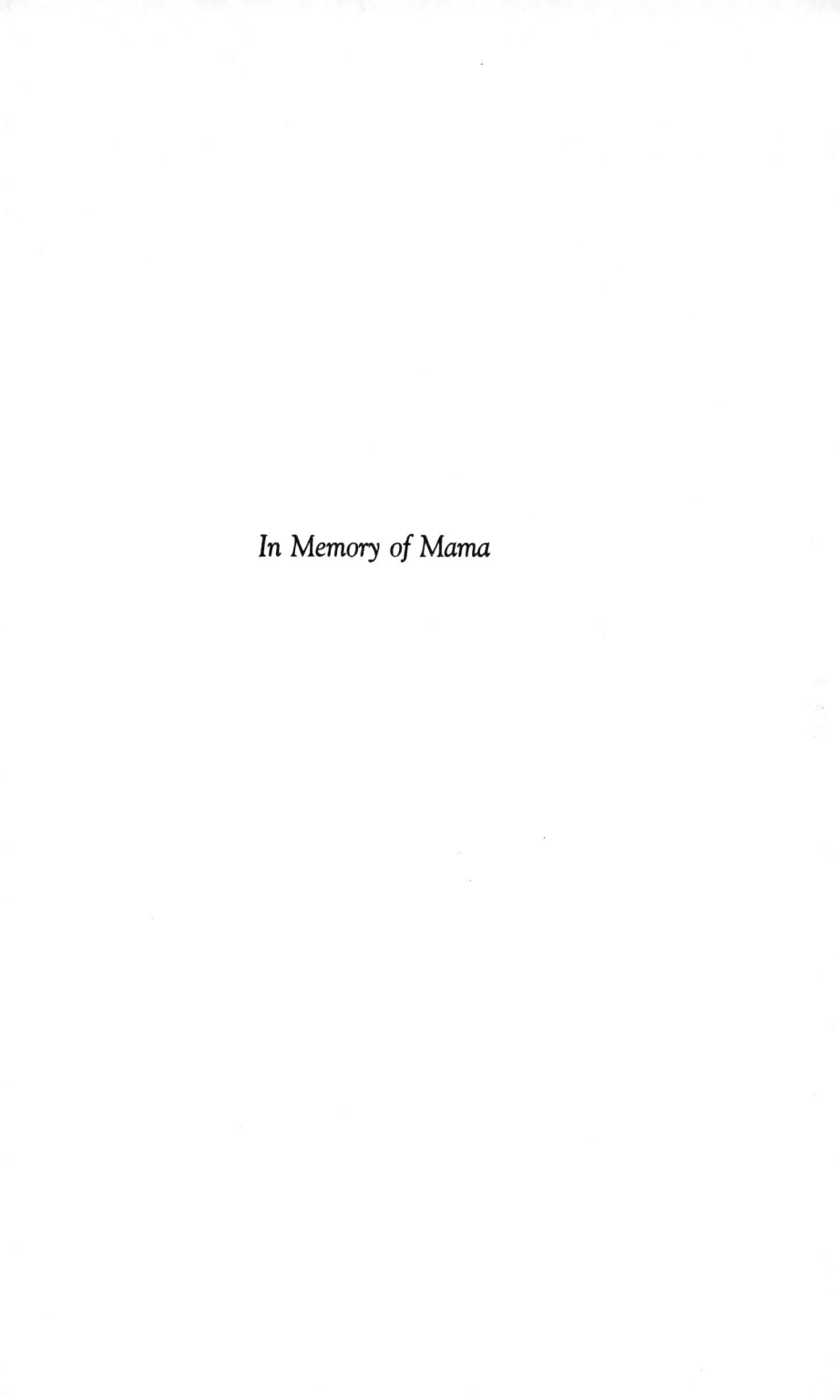

Contents

Prologue 9

Part 1 LOST AT THE CARNIVAL
1   Act Your Age 15
2   Good-bye, Mr. George 21
3   Fantasy 30
4   Going Back 34
5   Learning Seasons 41
6   Peace That Passes 49
7   That's Impossible 52
8   The Returning 56
9   Habits 62
10 Tears and Ice Water 64
11 Bumper Cars 68

Part 2 STUCK ON THE MERRY-GO-ROUND
12 The Pain 75
13 Flight 78
14 Strangers 82
15 Middle-age Miracle 88
16 From the Pages of 92

Part 3 SAFELY HOME IN LOVING ARMS
17 Love Messages 105
18 Finally 108

19	Already?	113
20	Joy	118
21	Leftovers	120
22	Father's Day Dog	125
23	Qualified?	131
24	Family	138
25	Voices from the Past	140
26	Love Room	146
27	Frugality	151
28	The Dreamer	153
	Epilogue	157

Prologue

Autumn was the season of the carnival when I was young. As summer ended, all the waking hours of my seven-year-old world were spent in anticipation of a trip to the carnival. And when our car finally pulled through the gates to the Attala County Fair, everything inside me came squealing alive!

I even forgot how tight my Sunday shoes were hugging my feet and Mama's anger about the tennis shoes I'd lost the day before. Nothing could spoil the excitement of the flickering lights—the grinding music.

My brothers ran on ahead of Mama and me as we walked toward the ticket booth. The night air brushed smells of peanuts and hot dogs and livestock stables into my nostrils. I could see the Ferris wheel glittering against the sky.

"Gonna be fun, huh?" Mama smiled down at me.

Before I could answer, a tall clown in red and black stopped in front of us. Without warning, like a jack-in-the-box, his big white face dipped down to mine. I shrieked, clinging to Mama. He laughed loudly and moved on.

But inside was a fairyland! We rode the merry-go-round

and ate cotton candy, and my brothers shot at rows of little ducks, trying to win a prize.

Somehow in the bustle of fun and people and sounds, I suddenly realized I had let go of Mama's hand. I spun around to find her but she was gone. My heart boomed like a drum. I was so frightened I didn't know which way to turn. All around me colorful rides danced up and down like gaudy Halloween masks, bleating down at me their music-box tunes. I could feel carousel horses prancing after me as I ran frantically back and forth, crying ... calling ... looking for Mama.

Then just as suddenly as I had become lost, the barker's chant gripped my attention. I stood statue still, entranced by the gibberish of a clown world. The magic, the pure delight of it all overwhelmed me and I wanted to stay forever!

But people kept laughing and talking and moving on by me and sawdust got in my eyes, spoiling the delicious feelings stirring inside. Loud, brassy music sent fearful thoughts calliopeing through me as I stumbled from one side show to another, hoping somebody would see me and recognize that I was lost.

Thirty years later I found myself in a different kind of carnival. It was my life! Happy, exciting, full ... lonely, frightening, empty. No patterns. No rules to follow. Everything just happened, with even more fury than before. In the trappings of endless charities, social and civic endeavors, the exhausting joys of Girl Scouts, Little League, and high school proms, I found myself on a merry-go-round ... bigger, faster, more exciting ... spinning, spinning, spinning, and I didn't know how to stop it to let myself off.

Yet after years of zooming in dizzy circles I didn't want

the merry-go-round to stop anymore. I didn't want to get off. I held on for dear life. The terrifying, confusing, exciting ride had become the only security I knew. I had even lost sight of God.

I couldn't imagine life without the demands of my family. I couldn't imagine myself anywhere else but on this ride, and being just a blur in the whirl of it didn't seem to matter. I was afraid to let go, afraid of change, afraid to trust Him.

But time would not wait and, too weak to keep holding on, I cried out for God's help.

The revelation that came was so lovely. I learned that He had been with me all along, allowing me to ride full gallop onto one rough course after another, and I became a little more sure of the turf with each stumble and fall. When I was able to listen for His guidance, the drunken ride began to slow down. The view of the world around me became easier to comprehend, and even gave me cause for rejoicing.

So come with me into the carnival of middle age. Come share the pain, the joy, and the absurdities of my own little side show. Perhaps it will give you some perspective on your own.

PART 1
Lost At The Carnival

1

Act Your Age

Comfort with any age never was mine ... just beyond my reach in the future; or locked, exaggerated, in my past.

On a hot Tuesday in August I became middle-aged. My husband George keeps telling me that nobody can move into a time bracket as vague as middle age on a given day.

But not only did it happen to me on a Tuesday in August, it happened between two-thirty and three o'clock in the afternoon. I remember glancing at the clock in the doctor's office when they called my name.

Lying there on the paper sheet, my feet securely fixed in stirrups, I stared at the blank white ceiling during the long wait for my gynecologist.

"It's good to see you again," he spoke down to me. He mentioned the heat, the need for rain. As he probed and peered, he asked how I'd been. Had my back been hurting? My legs? My stomach? No, I felt okay.

"That's good," he said, peeling off his disposable gloves and dropping them into a bright yellow pop-up-top can. "That's good," he repeated, closing the door behind him.

I waited again in his plush office while he shuffled medical records and mumbled something about the disarray of his desk. Young and handsome, my doctor friend must have felt very wise and even gentle as he leaned back in his genuine cowhide recliner watching me.

"Your uterus is enlarged," he said. "Much more than last year. I'd like you to consider a hysterectomy."

"A hysterectomy?" I echoed in surprise. "Hey look, I feel great!"

"Maybe so, but we'll keep an eye on it. Looks like trouble's ahead."

Hysterectomies happen to friends, I thought, not me. I don't even like the word "hysterectomy"—sounds so unproductive.

"What causes an enlarged uterus, anyway?" I asked quietly.

"Well, a lot of things can cause it," he said, leaning forward, resting his forearms on his desk. "You've had four children, for one thing." Then he smiled at me. *Compassionately*, I thought later. "But it's not uncommon for a middle-aged woman."

My ears started popping. I couldn't hear. I do that sometimes—go deaf when I'm embarrassed or scared. I knew he was still talking because I could see his lips moving, but only silence rang in my head. Finally I managed, "But is it uncommon to feel so good?"

"No, ma'am," he said. "It isn't."

"I'll think about it," I told him, then left quickly. In the elevator tears blurred the panel of buttons, so I poked at several, hoping one would get me to the ground floor. I didn't know why I was crying. *Maybe my back does hurt. Maybe there is pain in my legs. Maybe I don't feel so great.*

He said ma'am to me!

Never had anything so startled me as that label *middle-aged* and his deference to me. Of course I knew middle age was coming. I just hadn't expected it that day.

During my silent drive home I tried to smooth out the

muddled images that stuck in my mind about middle age. Gray hair. Wrinkles. Double chins. Age spots. All the negative attributes.

Yet I couldn't deny my chronological age. I *was* growing older! And I wasn't ready. I didn't know how to get ready or if I should even try. But my whole life seemed to change that day simply because a young doctor called me middle-aged.

Never a raving beauty, I'd still been content with my appearance. But now I seemed unable to control the desperation I felt, and the idea of looking young dominated my thoughts and actions.

First, I set out to charm George into believing we would be forever young—together. I lightened my hair, bought sexy nightgowns, and planned candlelight dinners for the two of us alone. When I walked down the street I pulled in my stomach, not breathing as I watched my reflection in the store windows. Any skin cream that mentioned youth, I bought. I joined a health spa, stayed on a diet, and even walked a mile and two-tenths each day. I bragged to my family about how great I felt, but more and more I seemed to be reclining, exhausted, on the couch.

One night as I scrambled through a box of old papers and mementos, looking for one of the children's birth certificates, I came across a picture of my mother. It was a snapshot George had taken shortly after the birth of our first child. My mother was such a handsome woman. I reckoned that at the time she must have been about my age now. I studied her likeness. Smiling proudly, she posed with her third grandchild.

Oh, Mama, I thought. *If being middle-aged bothered you, I never knew it.*

And there in the box next to her picture lay an old Tangee lipstick card, the staple that had held the lipstick still in place. *I wonder why I saved that?* There were no markings on the card.

And then I remembered. Lipstick was a status symbol. In my teen-age group, wearing lipstick meant a girl had "arrived." She was one of the "older" girls. I didn't arrive until I was fourteen.

I paused, remembering those trying, growing-up years so long ago ... the times before I was allowed to wear lipstick ... a shopping trip with Mama. I must have been just past my thirteenth birthday. A lump caught in my throat and tears filled my eyes as I remembered pleading with her to let me buy a tube of lipstick. It cost only twelve cents, but she said no. I cried. Thirteen years old and I openly cried.

When we got into the car, my tears still flowing, Mama turned to me. "Listen to me, honey," she said firmly. "It'll be a while before you'll be wearing lipstick. Now, you've got to learn to act your age. Here you are, wanting to be grown up enough to wear lipstick, yet you cry like a child because I won't allow it. It's important that you act your age! Remember that."

Yes, I do remember! I closed my eyes, holding the empty lipstick card and Mama's picture close to me as I cried. "Oh, Mama. I'm doing it again. I still don't know how to act my age."

Before I went to bed that night I slipped the picture in the corner of my bedroom mirror to remind me of Mama's admonition.

A couple of weeks later while sitting in church, I felt the preacher must have known about my turmoil, too. He preached on learning how to be content in whatever state we find ourselves.

Well, that sounded good. Sounded as if I should be content with middle age. But who can be content with falling apart, slowing down, looking old?

Then he said the key words! He said, "God has begun a good work in you, and He will perform it until it is finished. *Until it is perfected."*

A different perspective began tumbling slowly around in my head. Acting my age wasn't just a command of Mama's; it was a part of God's design for me. I touched my face to find a wrinkle. Could it be that I was not growing old at all—just being finished? Sounded great! And what's better still, *He* is in charge of the whole operation. I have only to go along with Him.

I shook the preacher's hand with vigor as we left the church and wondered if other middle-agers there had soaked up the good news same as I.

That night I seemed to fall asleep more peacefully than usual. Being "finished" certainly sounded like a better deal than "growing old."

I began to observe other middle-aged women more closely, studying their attitudes. Perhaps they too had been jolted by some young doctor, but more of them seemed unperturbed by double chins and bulging thighs and the years slipping by. In fact, they appeared to enjoy life as never before. Occasionally when a friend confessed to having some of the same fears I had, the edges of my discontent seemed to rest.

I kept trying to charm the father of my four grown-up kids, but most of the time I slept in granny gowns. I found I was comfortable, comfortable in granny gowns and becoming comfortable with my status of middle age.

But alas, perfection in me was far from accomplished. Staying comfortable with middle age day after dreary day proved to be an impossible task. Boredom was broken by a series of crises. Reminding myself daily that I wasn't getting old, just being perfected, worked on the ordinary days. But circumstances forced me to make changes. I faced more than double chins or bulging thighs.

In middle age I found I was just beginning to emerge from the chrysalis. It was quite a while later that I learned that being perfected means profound, painful changes. With the changes I began to see the possibilities God must see in people while He is fashioning them into finished, glorious creations.

2

Good-bye, Mr. George

*I thought of dying, yes . . .
But not of growing old.*

The old man sat across from me in the spacious lobby, his clean-shaven face folded with wrinkles. He glanced anxiously around the room as he rolled the brim of his gray felt hat with both hands.

Occasionally he swiped a hand across his mouth and fumbled at his shirt pocket as if a pen or his cigarettes should have been there, had always been there.

He was nervous. His feet moved awkwardly under the chair as he straightened the magazines into neat stacks on the table beside him. He didn't speak and when our eyes met, he didn't return my smile.

My husband was named for him, except that everybody called my father-in-law "Mr." George.

I had told him I was making arrangements for him to stay in the nursing home only until he recuperated from his week's stay in the hospital. But he knew more than a week of his life was being decided. He knew, yet he seemed too confused to understand fully and too frightened to protest.

As I waited for the administrator, I pondered all that had happened the weeks before. I resented George and his brother for leaving me this heartbreaking task. I resented "the system," a way of life with no better answer than nursing homes. I hated old age for taking away the comfort of able parents. My own parents had both died suddenly, before they were old. Now I questioned why God let people grow useless. Why was I caught in this trap with the sweet old man we called *Granddaddy?*

My husband's parents were gentle people, warm and unselfish. Their lives and their pride had been centered in their two sons and the grandchildren. I was the only in-law.

Mrs. Graham's senility came quickly. As if she wanted to withdraw from the world, she left us. Since she needed custodial care, the nursing home was the only alternative we had. I found I could accept that situation because she didn't seem really aware of what was going on.

But Mr. Graham was a different story. When the boys moved their mother to the nursing home and he came to stay with us, his world seemed to crumble and he never got it together again. After a couple of weeks he became ill and had to be hospitalized. Now the doctor said that he must be moved to a nursing home.

He knew he no longer had a voice in the matter. As I watched him across the room, I wanted to cry. I wanted to run away. I wanted to gather him in my arms and protect him from the world.

A young nurse called to me. "Mr. Miller will see you now."

I walked over to Mr. Graham. "I won't be long," I told him.

He seemed not to hear me. He made agitated, impatient gestures.

The administrator and I were finishing our consultation when a soft knock sounded on the door beside me. I knew it was Mr. Graham before I opened it. He stood silent, holding his hat over his chest with both hands. But it was the look on his face that still haunts me. His eyes begged.

He twisted his hat in his hands and whispered, "Let's get outta here."

I fended him off. "I'll be out in a minute."

He made exaggerated tugs, upping his trousers with one hand and then the other. He looked behind him and then back to me. His hands were trembling as he reached for his handkerchief. Before he could take it from his back pocket, tears began flowing down his face, and his thick lenses magnified the uncomprehending fear I could see in his eyes.

He shook with sobs as I put my arms around him.

"Don't do that, Granddaddy," I pleaded, trying to hold back my own tears. "Don't cry. It'll only be for a little while."

I nodded my thanks to Mr. Miller, then motioned to Mr. Graham, "Come on. Let's go have a look at your room."

He continued to cry as we followed the nurse. I shuddered as we passed through the halls. The odor of urine stung in my nostrils.

Old men, huddled close to themselves, crouched in wheelchairs or beds or in small groups, silent, waiting. Feeble hands reached out as we passed. I heard whispers and cries, and lonely, empty faces stared at me.

The nurse led us to a cubbyhole behind the nurses' station. His room was just large enough for a single bed and one chair. All the while she kept talking, assuring me he'd have a larger room as soon as one became available. And all the while my mind kept spinning, searching for a way to take him from that place, to manage somehow to keep him at home.

But I knew I couldn't. My husband traveled all week,

and his brother lived in Chicago. The children were in junior high and high school, and we didn't have an extra bedroom. For the few days Mr. Graham had been with us, it had been like having another child, except that his behavior was more unpredictable than that of a child's. His confusion kept me from ever resting. I had been afraid to go to sleep at night.

We stood in his room and talked for a long time, and gradually he calmed down as I assured him his stay was only temporary. Since we lived just a few blocks away I could visit him every day, I said.

For a time he seemed to be doing well, getting better.

I took him out often. We went to a local barber rather than have him wait in line for the barber at the nursing home. He laughed and joked with the barbers and I went down the street to shop.

When I returned he'd glanced nervously at me and fumbled at his pockets, embarrassed at having no money. I paid the barber while Mr. Graham stood behind me, acutely aware that, although I was spending his money, he felt like a charity case.

The next time we went out, I slipped a five-dollar bill in his jacket pocket. I was ready when his haircut was done.

"I think you put your money in your jacket pocket this morning," I told him.

He reached into his pocket and pride washed over his face as he pulled out the bill and waited for his change.

Once or twice a week I took him home for the night. He sat at my kitchen table, drinking coffee, as I prepared dinner. We talked about everything—about nothing. He was so grateful for anything I did for him. I was pleased to have him around, and he seemed to stop talking about "Mama" so much of the time.

But I began to notice that he was heavily sedated. When I took him home for the night, the nurses gave me drugs to give him "for restlessness." Although I didn't give them to him, he still slept a good deal. When I mentioned it to the nurses, they assured me the doctor did not over-prescribe drugs. I decided to let the issue drop, but reminded the nurses that if he needed me or wanted to see me for any reason, they were to call. They promised. Nevertheless, I visited him every day.

One afternoon when I arrived with his usual newspaper, I was startled to find him restrained in a wheelchair in the hall. Even the chair had been tied to the handrail. As I came nearer I could see him writhing, trying to free himself. He was muttering words I couldn't understand.

Frightened, I rushed to the nurses' station.

"What's wrong with Mr. Graham?" I demanded.

A fat little nurse's aide turned around quickly. "Oh, Mr. George has been a bad boy today."

"What d'ya mean?" I snapped at her.

"He set out to run away. Said he had to find you. But they tackled him right out there in the front yard. He never even made it to the street." She giggled.

The impact of her first words hit me, and I could hardly control my desire to strike her face. "What do you mean, 'Mr. George has been a bad boy'?" My voice rose. "Mr. Graham isn't a boy at all, young lady! He's an old man due your respect! How dare you refer to him as 'a bad boy'!"

A nurse stepped between us. "Don't get so upset, Mrs. Graham."

I turned my fury on her. "Well, I am upset! I'm not only upset, I'm so mad I'm ready to take on this whole nursing home!"

Everyone in sight froze, silent and blank. I slung the

newspaper across the floor and dashed back to Mr. Graham. I fumbled with his restraints. A nurse finally followed me.

"What are you doing?"

"I'm getting him outta here!"

"But you can't do that."

"Oh yes, I can."

"Well, that's all right," she stuttered. "I'll do that for you."

When I saw she was going to get him loose, I rushed to his tiny room. I piled his clothes in his luggage and pushed it into the arms of a bewildered orderly, one of many who'd gathered by this time to witness the scene. Obediently he took the suitcase to my car.

I braced Mr. Graham's drugged, weaving body against mine and as we wobbled down the long hall, I screamed at everybody and everything!

I took him home.

The kids, neither happy nor unhappy about Mr. Graham's return to our house that night, went about their usual routine, leaving me once again to ponder alone what to do. After Mr. Graham settled into a deep sleep, still overcome by the drugs, I eased out to sit on the back steps, hoping to get some perspective on what I had done—and what I would do next.

The cool, silent darkness hid me from the world and eased the feverish tears that washed freely down my face. I tried to think but my thoughts tangled into one another, rushing incoherently from options to plans to blank still places that felt suspended in permanent disrepair.

I tried to pray, but I couldn't identify what I should pray for. Doubled over close to myself, I pressed my arms against my stomach, trying to calm the jerking sobs that seemed to possess me. Try as I would to fight the confusion that swarmed through my head, I was unable to recognize that my anger was at old age itself—and at God for allowing that malady to ravage my world. I wanted Him to stop it ... to free Mr. Graham ... to ease the knots that kept gripping inside me. God seemed so indifferent and lost from me and I couldn't speak the words to summon Him. I could only huddle on the steps and cry.

Soon, or maybe much later, my writhing stomach rested and I went back inside. Still without a plan but curiously calm, I tumbled into bed and slept all night in sweet, exhausted, childlike sleep, unafraid and unconcerned about what to do in the morning. Surely my unuttered prayer had been heard, and He had given me a night of rest.

But as I watched Mr. Graham eating breakfast the next morning, I thought what a rotten thing old age had done to him, a man who'd worked hard all his life. His confident, sure steps had gone with time. His body and mind had broken down to a point that he was isolated from us. He was lonely, and no one could ease his loneliness.

Not even I.

This time I took him to a different nursing home. They were so good to him. He thought the dining hall was a restaurant and when I visited him, he'd invite me there and flag a passing nurse.

"Bring us two coffees please," he'd say.

"Yessir, Mr. George. Two coffees coming up."

They always humored him. With different treatment he adapted. Although still confused, he made the best of his situation. It helped me accept his acceptance.

Every Sunday George drove down to the nursing home to pick up his dad to spend the day with us. It soon became "Granddaddy's Day" and we settled into a routine. As the weeks and months wore on, I noticed how disturbed my husband seemed when he had to help his father do more and more little things for himself, like zipping up his jacket or tucking in his shirt. But being such a private man, so unlike me, he couldn't say it or cry about it or become angry. That seem like such a heavy burden for him to hold.

Each spring and fall for three years I took Mr. Graham on a drive up a nearby mountain. We saw the dogwood blooms spreading out across the valley in the spring, and watched the leaves turn red and gold in autumn time.

"Beautiful, isn't it?" I'd ask.

"Yeah, sho' is," he'd answer. "Wind's different here. Cooler." Then a faraway look would come over his face and he would be quiet, pensive, and shut up with his thinking. We sat in silence until it was time to go back.

Even after his death I drove up the mountain to see the seasons change, to breathe the mountain air, and to remember Mr. Graham.

In the end, the system had won. But I had won too. The old man who had sat nervously across from me that day in the nursing home lobby had taught me much about living.

I had resented being left to work out caring for him, but he and I had worked it out together. I still resent the system that depends on nursing homes to care for the aged, but I'm glad we found one of the better ones.

Old age made me the parent of my father-in-law. But the experience deepened my respect for his dignity. Even in his dependence he taught me the kind of tolerance which allows me to adapt to and even enjoy situations which I cannot change.

I cannot boast of faith so strong that fear of death eludes me. It does not. And old age is not a time of gold in my eyes. Sometimes my body shudders at thoughts of being helpless, of becoming the drooling child of my children, unaware.

Yet a quiet, gentle peace comes to me when I confess these fears to God. After all, He knows about my struggles and loves me anyway. Now as I pass through middle age and the steady advance toward my own death, I have assurance that He is ever with me.

Mr. Graham's decline and passing helped me to see more clearly God's hand in the pattern of life. And death.

Granddaddy, I love you.

3

Fantasy

If a fantasy world belongs to children, that explains my longing to be a child again.

It smelled of dust in the summer and burning hickory firewood in winter. The benches squatted, hard and square and brown with age. A certain kind of quietness brooded within its walls, as if someday God Himself might speak.

In its stark white country beauty, the little church sat piously on a hill overlooking our village. On Sunday mornings I raced my brother up the hill to ring the bell which let people all around know that it was time to meet to worship God again.

Every week I'd try to sneak to the back row with my classmates, but Mama always caught my eye. She'd glance at the empty seat beside her and I knew what she meant. But if Ma Tingle happened to be visiting us, I sat with her. Mama would always nudge my side if I dozed off to sleep, but Ma Tingle let me nestle close against her arm. Her smooth dress slipped warm against my face. She smelled like honeysuckle blossoms and baby powder, and the gold fillings in her teeth glistened when she smiled down at me.

I moved my small fingers over her thin soft hands and her wide gold wedding band, and we held the hymnal together when we stood to sing. She would let me wiggle back down into my seat when Mr. Summerhill prayed on

FANTASY

and on and on, my mind just full of wishing he'd hurry up and say amen.

Almost every summer the preachers stayed in our home during the revival at the church, even though our house was already running over with children (by the time I was ten, there were eight of us). Revival was a time of celebration for everybody in our community, and Mama went about the endless tasks with boundless joy and energy.

For days beforehand, everybody helped clean the church: washing the windows, sweeping the floors, and shaking the dust from the green grass curtains that divided the Sunday school rooms.

At home we stayed busy polishing silver, washing windows, and cleaning closets. We grumbled a lot about cleaning closets, not understanding the necessity of it since the doors were always closed anyway. But it was Mama's way, so we cleaned the closets.

Before the preachers came, she planned meals, got out her good china, and covered the dining room table with her best white linen tablecloth.

The dining room was my favorite room, and sometimes I'd slip inside the French doors and just stand there admiring its beauty, the sparkling silver and delicate china, perfectly placed on rich white linen. Smells of luscious red roses made my heartbeat quicken, waking my fantasy of eating in the presence of kings.

And the "preachers of the Word" were kings to my mind. Being the fifth child, I seemed always to be too old to enjoy the privileges of children and too young to participate in adult activities. Perhaps my yearning to eat in our majestic dining room with the great "men of God" was as much an effort to feel grown-up as it was the desire to hear their wise words. But unhappily, I ate in the kitchen. Sitting there on the bench, I'd catch a glimpse of the finery and hear snatches of their conversation every time the swinging pantry door opened. I imagined that someday I too would be allowed to sit on a warm, textured cushion of the highbacked chairs and listen to the wise men speak.

I did have a small part in our guests' comfort, however. We had only one bath, and it functioned well if the summer brought enough rain to keep the holding tank outside the bathroom window at a certain level. But if the water level got too low, my younger brother Max and I were the appointed water carriers. More often than not, we were called into duty.

Our job was to refill the toliet tank after each flush. Sometimes I can still see Max, curly topped and skinny, calling out to me: "Hey out there—he's doing it again! The preacher's doing it again!" Giggling, we'd grab our buckets and race across the pasture to the pump.

It was during the summer revival of my tenth year that I stepped shyly into the aisle and went forward, confessing my sins and asking Jesus to come live inside me. The next week I was baptized in McAdams pond and I felt all safe and sure and loved.

But even that didn't afford me much clout with the seating arrangement. There were just too many siblings who were older than I, and I never was permitted to eat with the preachers in Mama's dining room.

When I find time to reflect, I understand that it was a problem of space. Only eight could fit at the table. My feelings of being unacceptable and unworthy were only of my own imagining.

Even today when it was so easy to regret many things, I find myself wishing I had had the preacher come eat at our house when the children were younger. But we never had a dining room big enough nor attended a church small enough that preachers went home with members to eat.

Still, sometimes as we sit in the balcony at First Baptist Church in Atlanta, I glance down at all the beauty—curved comfortable pews, a full orchestra, a magnificent choir—and suddenly tears start pushing up in my eyes, threatening my Sunday morning makeup. Where is the smell of dust and musty air, the burning hickory firewood? I want to feel the hard square bench against my back and sing along with the untrained voices, *Bringing in the Sheaves.*

And Mr. Summerhill . . . I'd like to hear him pray again so I could be still and listen. But most of all in my fantasy I turn and say to George, "The preacher's coming home with us for lunch today."

Then I smile at my mature childishness. The preacher doesn't even know me. We number in thousands here. I shake my head to clear my mind.

Yet I am still the little girl in shoes too tight, standing inside the French doors looking at Mama's table with rich white linen, delicate china, and sweet red roses.

Now in middle age I have several options. I can accept the unfulfillment of the past or I can continue to fret. I can let go the dream . . . which seems like the reasonable, middle-aged thing to do.

But no . . . I think I'll just send him an invitation. Yes, I'll have all the children come home. Set up two tables. I can get out my good china; polish the silver. I'll need another white tablecloth, though. Maybe buy some red roses and . . .

4

Going Back

*Catch an autumn leaf, little girl, little girl.
Turn around, turn around and you'll be home.*

I read the letter once again, stuffed it into my jeans' back pocket, called the dogs, and headed along the path down to the creek. The fresh greenery of summer had gone, and the back porches and patios of other houses on other streets pushed unwelcome images through the naked trees. *My little woods—my place to run to—it's no longer all mine.*

But wild fern still decked the creek bank, and tiny, funny-faced flowers held bright yellow glows, their fragile stems stretching between tree roots. The dogs still went happily about splashing in the cool water.

I sat on my log and took out the letter again. *Twenty-fifth reunion.*

Has it really been twenty-five years?

Yes. Of course. And I will be going back.

A foolish kind of elation zinged through me. It felt childish, tingling, exciting. Back to Kosciusko!

In my mind's eye I saw the little Mississippi town, named back in the 1800s for a Polish general and proudly proclaimed each week by the *Star Herald* as the "Bee Hive of the Hills."

When I was young and autumn came to Kosciusko, time moved from sulky to impatient. The lazy pace of summer turned to bustling as if preparing hurriedly for a bitter winter. The shops and stores around the square redressed their windows with colorful displays of back-to-school shoes, pencils, and paper. Cones of new fabrics spanned out across W. C. Leonard's department store windows with Rothmore coats and McCall patterns.

Standing on the steps of the majestic courthouse, one could hear fragments of band music catching in the wind as "Kosy" High prepared for the year's first football game. Leaves piled along the wide, hilly streets smoked out a sweet, telling incense of the new season. On the earliest frost-tinged mornings, dizzy shades of yellow and brown splotched the oaks and sycamore trees, and red and orange blazed the maples. People on the sidewalk moved briskly, their faces showing happy inebriation. The town's inhabitants seemed drunk on the beginnings of school and football and trials up at the courthouse.

The energy and elation carried through the gray evenings with threatening clouds and katydids scratching in the coming dark, as children romped in front yards, catching balls, chasing and squealing and laughing. Mothers called in their young, and the town settled down, acknowledging the death of another sweet, unforgettable summer.

But I wouldn't be going back just to see autumn. I was going back to school. Transported over twenty-five years past, I could feel my face freshened by the crisp morning air. The cotton gin hummed, and sharp pinging rang out from Mr. Cook's blacksmith shop. I hurried to catch the yellow school bus for the three-mile ride into town.

Juggling books and handbag, holding on to the pole behind the bus driver, I held my head as still as possible in order to keep my carefully combed hair in place. My best friend, Snooks, got on at the next stop, and she and I gossiped with Jean and our other friends as we swayed forward and back with each downshift. We rode over the Yockanookany River every day (noticing it only when it was swollen) and on into town.

At the high school, we climbed two flights of wide, oil-swept stairs to our third-floor homeroom. During study periods our group of girls gave Miss Green, the librarian, a hard time, whispering, carelessly replacing books, giggling at her dark, angry eyes.

In spite of her fussing, we knew she liked us. Saying she would kill us if she knew, some of us sneaked down to her house one night and watched her say good night to her date. We managed to go lots of places in Rose Ann's little 1928 roadster with a rumble seat and a sign on the back proclaiming "All boys who smoke, throw your butts in here." It was the most risqué thing we ever did.

I jerked out of my reverie, feeling a great longing. *Yes. Oh yes, I must go back!*

Nearly all of our class did go back for that reunion. The little town drew us to her like a mother hen, wings outstretched and waiting. From the West Coast to the East, from South and North we came, drawn by a force I couldn't understand. As George and I drove out of Georgia, across Alabama, and onto the soil of our birth I tried to identify that force, that pull that made me happily willing to drive hundreds of miles for a few hours of fellowship at a high school reunion.

"Why do you suppose people do it?" I asked George.

He thought for a moment, then smiled. "To see who looks the oldest, I reckon. Or the youngest."

I said, "No, but maybe. Maybe just to show off photographs of our beautiful daughters and handsome sons, hoping someone will see a resemblance of our youth." For twenty-five years most of us had lived in different worlds, yet for this specified evening we came together again.

George was right. Everybody there looked older. Then I noticed a childhood friend who had gone all the way through school with me. She was trying to read my name tag. How awful! She didn't even recognize me!

After the shock, I moved from group to group, talking, laughing, remembering. Someone read excerpts from the *Kosy-Hi-Daze*—gossip and quips about who's dating whom. The delicious feeling of coming back home stayed with me all evening.

Members of the class had prospered well. There were doctors, lawyers, preachers, teachers, housewives, and business executives. Miss Green would have been impressed, I thought. My high school sweetheart still looked good, more mature and confident. We talked about our children, about our teen-aged "love affair."

I glanced across the room to see George standing among friends but looking at me. His dark eyes quietly held my face the way they had so long ago and I loved him again—the giddy, urgent kind of love I had felt at seventeen. He had been in college, older, wiser, a "man of the world," I thought then. But he was more handsome now, still impeccably dressed. His smile still spread quickly across his face.

My old friend grinned at me. "I kept hanging around thinking you'd leave George," he teased.

I laughed at his flattery. "Well, sometimes I sure have thought about it. But I just stayed on. You know, to make his life full of joy and all."

"Yeah, I got a woman like that too."

"She's good to you?"

"Yes. She's really a great girl."

"I'm glad. And it's good to see you again."

"You too," he said, and we drifted into separate groups again.

Standing away from the crowd, I felt the question tugging at me again. *Why are we all here? Why did we make the effort, and why do I feel so good with them?* There was an energy among us, an aura around us, and we melded into something that I had once known.

I wanted to bottle up the feeling and take it home with me. It was as though all the problems since I left school didn't matter. But I knew none of us could really go back to take up life as it had been.

The faces had changed and so had the town. O. K. Power's Ford was gone from the square and Boyd's Drug Store no longer had a soda fountain. And the end of the old drive where I used to wait for the school bus had grown up in weeds, and Mr. Cook's Blacksmith was shut down forever.

As George and I drove out of Kosciusko the next morning on the beautiful Natchez Trace, we looked again for landmarks, all different now. And we looked again at one another, remembering that we had fallen in love on this very same road.

Under construction during those years, the Parkway had been where most young lovers ended up on Friday and Saturday nights. We parked along the sandy roadbed to talk, to smooch, or to meet with other couples. We turned our radios to WLAC and Gene Noble's playing of the latest hits from Randy's Record Shop in Gallatin, Tennessee. It had been such a peaceful time in our lives. It seemed so easy to be in love.

"You don't look twenty-five years older," George said and touched my face.

"But I am."

"Just in your mind," he said. "You don't look older to me." He touched my face again, and I knew that he didn't see me growing older, and it made me warm.

Back in Georgia, it rained every day the next week, certainly not the kind of weather to help overcome my letdown blues. George had to go out of town, and I moped about the house, puzzled. The reunion still hung in my mind, the filling need of it, the fleeting time of it.

For a while I struggled with envy over the exciting career one friend had told me about. I kept recalling certain conversations, wishing I'd said this instead of that and had asked why instead of how. If it were to do over, I'd buy a really smart outfit, regardless of the budget. After all, it was my day, wasn't it?

I remembered my private struggle for acceptance in high school—Do they really like me? Are my clothes right? My hair? Will I be invited? Those desperate cries for recognition flooded my memory.

Maybe if I write a great novel they'll be really impressed at the next reunion. Who knows, maybe I'll even write a movie. And go back to Kosy for the filming. Right there on the town square. Bet that'd knock 'em on their heels.

Oh dear, I thought. I'm still responding in the same old way, thinking I need to attain success to be recognized and accepted.

But going back to see my classmates had made me realize that success or failure really had nothing to do with their acceptance of me now. Like a giant womb, the old town had held us all in her warmth, nurtured us, molded us, and helped us grow. Even when the time came and we pushed free to live our separate lives, we took with us a likeness of one another—a likeness that would always bind us in a kindred spirit.

SEASON OF THE CARNIVAL

The elusive joy I had felt that night was the sweet renewal of the bond that once bound us.

5

Learning Seasons

There seemed no time for dreams when I was newly middle-aged. Crisis followed crisis with the children, who were not always a source of pride and pleasure. Each one of their crises led me into still another season of the carnival.

When I awoke that Wednesday morning the storm had ended, but rain still fell in gentle whispers outside my window. I could hear the swollen creek's rushing. Always after a heavy rain it swirled and twisted, slapping at itself, rushing to somewhere, heaven knew where.

I sat up in bed. *I'm like the creek*, I thought as I glanced at the clock. *Eight o'clock! Is that all?* I fell back in bed, pulling the sheet over my head. *I can sleep as long as I want. Today the kids got their day started on their own.*

Hugging a pillow, I curled close to myself and went back to sleep.

I usually had premonitions, especially about the children. George didn't believe in premonitions, and I could never understand why since mine were so accurate most of the time. Years of mothering and coping and busy schedules had sharpened my feel for the unexpected.

But that morning I had none. I could only feel the soft, sweet-smelling sheets against my skin, the stillness of the room, the delicious quiet of the morning.

Peace, like in the song, filled up my senses all that day

long. When nighttime came again, I lay down unaware of what the next hours would bring.

"Mrs. Graham, this is Cobb General Hospital. Your son, Marcus, has been in an accident. We need your permission to treat him."

My mind struggled out of sleep. "Is he hurt?" I asked, immediately realizing the absurdity of the question.

"We don't know how badly he's hurt."

"I'll be there as soon as I can."

I looked at the clock. Twelve o'clock was official curfew time for our seventeen-year-old. It was twelve-thirty. *Marc should have been home thirty minutes ago and it's pouring down rain out there again.*

Lisa and Lindsay called upstairs at the same time. "What's the matter, Mama?"

"It's Marcus. He's been in an accident."

The girls scrambled for clothes and rain gear while I dressed with unreasonable calm. George was in Washington. It didn't occur to me that Marc was seriously injured. He had walked away from his only other automobile accident just a year before with a few minor scratches. He had totalled the car and the police shook their heads: "It's a miracle he survived at all," one officer told George.

I suppose I thought Marcus was indestructible. But as I rambled in the closet for a misplaced shoe, I looked for a scapegoat. *George, why is it that every time a trauma occurs in this family you're not here?*

No, it wasn't George's fault.

As I searched for my car keys on the desk in the kitchen, I noticed my Bible still open. Just hours before I had asked God to take care of Marc. *Now look what's happened, God.*

I flipped the Bible closed and picked up the car keys.

LEARNING SEASONS

The girls and I didn't talk on the way to the hospital. The windshield wipers were beating out a hollow kind of rhythm as I struggled to see the road through the blinding rain. What a night for an accident, I thought. What a night to face more trouble. Trouble ... my father's words came back to me. "Trouble's God's schooling and one learning season just ain't enough."

How many learning seasons will be mine, Lord?

We still sat in the hushed waiting room at two o'clock in the morning. An old man huddled in a far corner, hugging his crutches. Two teen-aged boys argued quietly beside the telephone booth. Wrestling with her small child, a young mother chain-smoked and coughed. Lisa and Lindsay sat across from me. We didn't speak. Sometimes we smiled at one another—nervous, comforting kind of smiles. There was nothing to say now. Just the waiting ... the numb waiting.

About two-thirty a nurse told me the doctor would talk with me soon. *Why is it taking so long? Surely if he's hurt badly they would have told me. The nurses look so calm. One had already told me she thought Marcus could go home with us.*

Still we waited.

At three-fifteen the doctor came out.

"Mrs. Graham, we're moving Marcus to intensive care." Then he paused, looked away from me and back, his young face soft and gentle. "The truth is, Mrs. Graham, Marcus is just so drunk we don't know how seriously he's hurt."

My heart began pounding so hard I thought it would surely leap from its cage. I'd never seen him drunk and I hadn't wanted to even think that he drank. I couldn't speak.

"He has a collapsed lung," the doctor went on, "but I

think he'll be okay. His teeth are really messed up. Probably lose three or four lower ones.

"I've called in a diagnostician. Probably be awhile before we know how badly he's hurt. I don't think he's critical. He's talking some. You may see him for a few minutes if you wish."

When I went in I became frightened for the first time. Marcus was propped in a sitting position, chest bare. White heart-monitor discs were stuck to him and a drain hung from his side. There was an IV in one arm and a tube inserted through his nose into his stomach. One large tube was pushed directly through his chest to his lung.

Marcus's neck and face were swollen, his mouth blue. His blond hair looked almost white, as pale as his skin. He opened his eyes briefly and I touched his arm.

His skin flinched as if my touch were painful. "Marcus," I said softly. "How you feeling?"

My son's eyes opened again and tried to rest on my face. "Like s   ," he slurred at me.

Stunned by his words, I backed away from his bed. I couldn't believe what I had heard—the pain of it crawled inside me. He had never spoken to me like that—never dared be so disrespectful.

Suddenly nauseated, I escaped.

Standing outside the door, I couldn't cry. *Oh God, that's not my child in there! He's someone I don't even know. He can't be my son!*

But he was my son and my revulsion gave way to anxiety. *He's hurt really bad. I don't want him to die!*

I telephoned George and the sound of his voice comforted me. He caught the next plane back to Atlanta. I had called his brother earlier and he'd come to wait with us.

For four days we were allowed five minutes with Marcus three times each day. His words were always the same. "My neck hurts so bad."

Every minute of every day I argued with God ... making bargains, trying to impose my own will on Him. I wanted our son to live. I thought God's will was for him to die.

On the fifth day, George and I had barely arrived home when we were summoned to come back to the hospital. Panic filled me. I was certain Marc had died or was near death. *What if they are being kind, and they will give us the bad news at the hospital rather than on the telephone?*

Neither of us spoke a word on the return to the hospital. My mind dug up memories of our little boy who had grown up to be such a handsome seventeen. Our little boy, who charmed and frustrated his teachers from grade one ... spending much of his time in the principal's office for pranks; who doubled his allowance by buying candy and balloons and selling them at school. Our little boy who thought he was in this world only to make money and have fun.

At twelve he mowed lawns and washed dishes at a restaurant after school. At fourteen he bought himself a Honda and at sixteen, his own car. His pride was not in the ownership but the fun that came with having these things.

His grades were good, then bad. No consistency. His peers, looking as unkempt as he, dictated his lifestyle, which included long hair and arguments about curfew. He never gave a thought to the future.

Does he have a future, Lord? Even with the difficulties we still love him. Please let him live.

When we reached the intensive care unit, my heart was

racing. This is the way you feel, I thought, when someone tells you your child has died. My heart seemed to be pumping blood in and out of my veins in hard, swift spurts. Full ... then empty, then full again.

The nurse told us that the doctor had discovered that Marcus's neck was broken. They needed our consent for the surgery.

I sat down quickly in a nearby wheelchair and began to cry. George turned to me, as did the nurse, asking what was wrong. How could I explain the anxiety I had experienced those minutes since their call? My tears were tears of relief.

We signed the papers and waited again.

Two hours later a doctor came to tell us how it was going. He said he couldn't believe the boy was still alive, having been moved so many times in the five days after the accident. "A miracle," he said.

Thank You, God, for miracles. Thank You for that.

But the doctor cautioned us that Marc was still in danger. The slightest movement in the wrong direction could cut off his breathing, and he would die within a few seconds.

When he was finally wheeled out of the operating room, I caught my breath sharply and eeked out a little cry of disbelief. George, experiencing the same shock, looked at me.

This only son of ours, whose long hair had been our "thorn in the flesh" for over two years, was now as bald as Yul Brynner! They had shaved his head completely. Then we both laughed softly. It was good to laugh.

He was placed in fixed traction. Holes had been drilled in his skull on both sides and tongs were inserted, holding weights that hung behind the bed.

Five weeks later he graduated to a metal collar and we brought him home in a body brace from his head to his hips. He wasn't allowed to remove it even to take a bath.

Thus began another wait.

That fall was to have marked his senior year in high school. He was provided a homebound teacher and he studied a lot, but he was lonely. His moods were deep, brooding ones, and he snapped at me every time I turned around. I found it almost impossible to please him. My fear of his dying had turned into a frustration over his tedious living.

I changed the TV channel a hundred times a day for him. I cooked the meals he wanted. I handed him things. My six-foot kid-man was running me to death. I loved him and was thankful for his life being spared, but I was running low on patience.

Winter came and went. In the spring, Marc reached a new low, and so did I. Much of the time I was tired and irritated with his demands. He seldom talked about how he felt. He seldom talked to me at all, and I resented his silence.

But we had a celebration the day the doctor removed the brace after thirteen long, weary months.

In September Marcus entered Georgia State University. He took a full load. He also took to the tennis courts. He played tennis in the morning, the afternoon, and at night. When we got his first quarter grades we realized that while his tennis game had shown considerable improvement, his academic endeavors were dragging the net. The accident hadn't slowed him down at all, for he was back to the same old game—irresponsibility and fun.

But his grades improved during winter quarter. Just days before the end of that school year, he sat at the kitchen table as I made a cake. He spouted about a really "neat" professor who had it all together. I listened half-heartedly.

"Mother, you know, I never gave a serious thought to what I'd do with the rest of my life until I had that accident."

My ears perked up. The boy was saying something sensible.

"What'd you say?" I wanted to hear it again.

"Well, 'til I had that wreck I didn't have a plan of any kind in mind. Thirteen months is a lot of thinking time."

"What'd you think about?"

"Oh ... about what I wanted to do when it was all over."

"What'd you decide?"

He cocked his head in thought for a moment. "Haven't decided yet. I'm still thinking." He plopped his empty milk glass on the cabinet. "But at least now I know there's a plan out there somewhere. I never knew that before."

As he grabbed his tennis racket and left, I wanted to give him a hug. But I didn't. I turned back to my cake.

He's got a plan? How marvelous!

At least he's thinking, Lord. At least he's thinking.

I looked out the window and noticed tiny new leaves beginning to hug the tall naked trees.

Spring already. Fresh, beautiful spring. I just wonder, Lord, how much learning You've got laid out for us this season?

6

Peace That Passes

It happens every year at Christmas time—this feeling cavorting through the house like time just lost its place and the kids are kids again. A fever of excitement, a spirit of gladness which I cannot explain swells into the air.

Tonight is Christmas Eve, and sounds of their voices, their laughter and music drift into my kitchen. A luscious apple cake cools on the rack and the turkey is ready for the oven. I'm chopping onions and celery and peppers for our celebration dinner tomorrow.

Icy crystals form outside the window, and twilight seems to hold the trees and shrubs like frozen shadows in our back yard. But in the den a fire burns steadily, licking and popping at the hickory logs and I am warm.

The children's laughter rings out again.

What is it about this time of year that brings us all such pleasure? Why does every sound seem so precious, so good?

Each of us has already opened our one package according to our Christmas Eve tradition, and still they linger, admiring, reminiscing about other gifts and other Christmas Eves.

I stop my chopping and stare down at the round white onion in my hand.

"It's real," I say aloud. "This feeling is as real as this onion, yet it has no name. No shape. No smell."

I turn and lean against the cabinet to listen more intently, trying to capture the fullness of the moment.

SEASON OF THE CARNIVAL

Is it freedom? Could our Christmas celebration give us such freedom—elate our spirits so?

The tree lights flash their silent colors, opening up the darkness with shimmering tinsel and fragile balls and angel hair. Pretty wrappings and ribbons hide more surprises under the Christmas tree, and the smell of freshly cut cedar fills my head.

They laugh again—contented, delighted laughter, like children with new toys.

Is it the Christ child—the Savior, who came into this world like children everywhere? Could our joyful praise in remembrance of His birth give us permission to be children again?

Of course! We're all children to God.

I glance around the door and smile at them, then get back to my chopping. That explains my whimsical behavior today, I keep thinking, pleased to note my day did have some logic.

Everything started out normally enough this morning on my usual frantic last minute shopping jaunt. As I made my way through the crowded store, trying to reach sporting goods, I sought a short cut through the toy department. But shopping carts and other frantic mothers blocked the aisle so I pushed up against the doll display to wait my exit turn.

Suddenly my eyes locked on three baby dolls, all huddled together on the shelf like frightened little sisters, each small hand reaching out to touch the other. Their rosy cheeks shined—their round wide eyes smiled at me. Two were blonde, wearing pink nightgowns. The dark-haired one wore blue and all three were wrapped in soft flannel blankets.

Even after the aisle had cleared, I stood there staring, wishing my girls were little girls again. I realized, with regret, that baby dolls for high school and college students would be inappropriate. As I walked away, I reached out to touch them.

I bought all three!

7

That's Impossible

Shock resistant though I am, my label also warns to handle with care.

The fourth year after my dramatic entry into the world of middle age, I went for my annual gynecological checkup. In the lavishly decorated waiting room, strains of Bach added to the ambience I felt as I glanced through the month-old *Good Housekeeping* magazine.

There I sat, a middle-aged woman, in a room filled with smiling young ladies caressing their bulging stomachs. Even the young nurse was pregnant, a living advertisement.

Through the years I'd mastered the art of filling the urine specimen cup. I still didn't like the needle prick in my finger. But off with the clothes, on to the table with paper sheets. Knees up, feet in stirrups, the long wait.

I held my "on the mark, get set" position through the doctor's examination. When he told me what he'd found, I was ready to "go"!

He stood beside me, looking down at me with caring eyes. I watched his thick, dark beard flinch slightly as he spoke quietly. "Mrs. Graham, I believe that you're about three months pregnant."

I came up from the table with a dry heave in my throat. "Don't tell me that!"

"But I'm afraid it's true," he said.

Then I began to cry. The doctor stood by helplessly. I explained to him, between sobs, why it couldn't be true. "You see, I can't have a baby. Not now. You know? I'm middle-aged. There's just no way I can handle having another baby now. My kids are grown up, don't you see? I just can't."

I kept talking, trying to persuade him to rescind his statement. "If I were younger, maybe. But I'm just too old, don't you understand?" It sounded more as if I were trying to excuse myself from a WMU panel at the church than to back out of a pregnancy.

He handed me tissues as I wiped away tears and mascara and any sign of makeup I had covered my middle-aged lines with that morning. It was the first time I'd ever seen a doctor who wasn't in a hurry. He just stood there, handing me tissues, handing me tissues. I wanted to snatch the whole box from him and blame somebody.

"I know how you must feel," he said at last, not unsympathetically. Of course he didn't know, but he was pale and serious. Not only was he not in a hurry, he didn't seem to know what in the world to do. It was terrible. Who wants a doctor who doesn't know everything?

But he did tell me he would do a "two hour UCG" to be positive about his diagnosis. The test would, however, take several hours to run since the lab was so busy. I agreed when he assured me he would call as soon as he got the results.

I left his office feeling considerably heavier than when I had come.

At home I sat quietly in the den, feeling cocooned, wrapped into myself as I had twenty years before during my other pregnancies. I couldn't think about this or anything; my mind had suddenly lost its place.

The telephone jangled loudly, piercing my isolation. It was my auditor husband calling to say he was going out of town.

"How 'bout getting my shirts ready? I've got to be in Montgomery by four."

As George packed I said, "The doctor told me this morning that I'm three months pregnant."

"What does he know?" He laughed. "You know better than that."

"I didn't say it, the doctor did!"

He laughed again. He took the shirts off the hangers and ignored me as if I hadn't even been pregnant when I had ironed them. He had turned my trauma into a joke and when he drove away, I slammed his shoes against the door.

I called my friend Kathleen. We sat at the kitchen table waiting for the doctor's call, as we drank leftover coffee and ate stale crackers. We talked, almost in whispers, about things like maybe it was God's will that I should have another child and how we felt about abortions and how older parents must readjust their lives.

I began to feel like Abraham's Sarah. The whole concept was absurd. Maternity dresses, baby diapers, first grade plays, preteen music, teen-ager woes! No! No! No! Just thinking about it scared me silly, I wished I were back in the hands of that fresh young gynecologist who had recommended a hysterectomy. Boy, would I ever listen to him!

Kathleen tried to comfort me with gentle words. Then she looked helplessly at me and lamented, "I know you must feel just awful."

Then I cried again.

THAT'S IMPOSSIBLE

The telephone rang! I knocked over a chair, spilled coffee, and tripped on a stool, reaching the receiver before the second ring.

"Yes, yes," I said anxiously, ignoring trivial things like "Hello."

"The test is negative, Mrs. Graham," he said.

I wanted to shout, but I cried again—with joy! I giggled, then cried some more. "Thank you, Doctor. Oh, thank you so much."

"The test is negative this time, Mrs. Graham, but we've got to consider a hysterectomy now."

"I will!" I told him. "I will. I really will."

I changed doctors instead.

8

The Returning

After two years of working hard to impart her musical knowledge to over 175 seventh- and eighth-graders, Lisa quit. Just like that! When she called to tell me she said, "Mother, I can't do it anymore."

I begged her to reconsider. "What will you do?"

"I'm taking a job in Alabama," she told me happily. "Selling insurance."

Lisa sell insurance? Never! "George, what will we do about her?"

Calmly he said, "What can we do?"

Six months later in January, she called to say she could not sell insurance, and she was broke. "We'll come get you," I told her. But before the day was over, I was having second thoughts about stepping in to rescue her.

Lisa had been a headstrong, self-confident child, and a teen-ager generally more concerned with her own needs than anyone else's. She wasn't disobedient, yet she seemed determined to do everything her own way. My mother used to say that Lisa was just like me, with my stubborn drive. We had not had real problems getting along, but I knew the Lisa who came back to us would not be the same as the girl who left home six years before to go to college.

Many of our friends had experienced grown children returning to the nest because of economics, and all of them declared if it were to do over again, the children wouldn't move back. But I felt we had no choice.

As we drove to Alabama to move Lisa back, George and

THE RETURNING

I rationalized how nice having her home again would be. Lindsay had never really known her older sisters Laura or Lisa since she was so much younger. In that respect we agreed that having Lisa there with Lindsay would be pleasant.

Lindsay was indeed happy to have her sister home again. Things began to settle down, and it looked as if all might quietly fall into place.

Lisa and I talked openly about our arrangement with what I called reason. First, we agreed that her stay with us was temporary. Second, she was to be a guest in our house. Since Lindsay occupied her old room, Lisa gladly took a smaller bedroom. And we agreed to be considerate to one another.

Lots of agreements were made.

But Lisa had not been home three days before I knew we were both in for a restless winter. She was tired and irritable. I was irritable, too. By this time I'd allowed myself to become resentful. Laura had just finished school, Marcus was still in college, and Lindsay was a senior in high school. Money was tight, and I felt imposed upon.

My resentment built. After all, we had done for her what we should do: put her through college. Now Marc and Lindsay should have my attention and energy.

The worst part was that Lisa couldn't find a job. Although she had her degree, teaching music was all she had done, and she vowed she would never teach again. After two weeks of interviews she realized she wasn't prepared to go to work in the business world.

She had to do something. She had car payments and other obligations. We could not contribute to any of her money needs. Her room and board alone were putting a strain on us. My resentment came more because she had not heeded my advice than because of the inconvenience. We clashed, my stubborn will not letting me forget that she could have still been gainfully employed; hers doggedly claiming that it had not been a mistake to quit. In fact, she never seemed to regret at all giving up her position as a teacher.

So, we had blowups over little things. We pouted about bigger things. I sensed that she was so caught up in her own shame, her embarrassment at what she thought was failure, that her one consuming goal was to get a job and be on her own again. And I understood the humiliation of being dependent on us again.

Sometimes I admired Lisa, even envied her spunk in making such a drastic change in her life, giving up her teaching career which she had thought she most wanted to do. I admired her unrelenting search for independence from us again. She took a job as a waitress at a Ramada Inn and started back to school to study business. After working eight hours every day, she would come home, change clothes, and rush off to class. Even with such a grueling schedule, her determination never faltered.

In September Lindsay left for school and Lisa seemed moody, lost without the sister who had become her good friend. Then this lovely daughter who caused me such anxious moments became a source of pleasure to me. We had long talks, lazy dinners alone when George was out of town. She shared her hopes, and sometimes we were even able to discuss our frustrations over her situation.

After two quarters of going to school and working too, the strain began to show. She was physically spent, mentally drained, and emotionally depressed. Even though I'd often sit and cry helplessly, hurting for her, my concern did not prevent us from quarreling more. Hostility kept building, just as my friends had predicted. Sometimes Lisa seemed more selfish than I had ever remembered her being, and I responded with anger.

One Saturday morning she got up early to help me put the house in order. She was busily doing first one thing and then another. It was good to see her energetic and uplifted. When she started a load of laundry, I thought, *How sweet of her to help me.*

But after the clothes were put in the dryer, I realized she had washed my best nightgown with the white clothes in bleach. Worse, she had then tossed it into the dryer. The gown had been a Christmas gift from George, and I loved it. It came out of the dryer shrunken and bleached to a dirty tan-white.

I cried and yelled at Lisa for her carelessness. She tried to apologize but in frustration I wouldn't let her. Finally she got in her car and left. As soon as she pulled away from the driveway, remorse overtook me. I was ashamed that I had acted so ugly. Now she was gone and I couldn't apologize. The first day in weeks she had been really happy, and I had ruined it.

More pressing than the regret for my behavior was my concern for where she had gone. With its usual vigorous guilt for fuel, my mind went into overdrive. I imagined that something terrible was happening to her. Maybe she would be killed in a car wreck, and I'd never get to tell her how sorry I felt. I recalled her depression. Would she be so hurt that she'd run away, be angry with me forever? Terrible images kept racing through my head. I asked God to forgive me and promised Him I would ask her forgiveness, too, if He would just bring her home safely.

Three hours later my stomach still writhed with the gnawing anxiousness I always felt when scared or worried—or suffering from the pain I'd caused someone else. When I heard her car door slam, relief settled over me like a warm blanket. *At last! She's okay!* I rushed from the kitchen to apologize.

Then I noticed she had a Rich's department store bag in her hand and I recoiled. *She's just been shopping! She never has any money as it is. How could she be so foolish to spend money just because she's mad?*

I turned and flounced back into the kitchen, giving no thought to my prayerful promises.

That night when I opened my dresser drawer, I saw folded neatly on top of the faded gown the most beautiful thing I had ever seen. It was rich beige satin with soft lace, far more lovely and expensive than the one it replaced. I cried, for many reasons. I knew she didn't have the money to spare to buy it. I knew I had been wrong to condemn her, and I cried because I realized she was not totally self-centered. She had a sweet, giving spirit. I don't think I ever felt so badly, so guilty about anything in my whole life. Nor do I remember ever loving her so much. Only later, further into middle age, did I realize that she could have chosen to fight defensively. Instead, she made an endearing gesture of love.

Eight months later Lisa had fallen in and out of love three times. Her car had seemed to be on the blink constantly. One night she even got a speeding ticket on her way home from school. But she had acquired excellent skills in business and some confidence.

Then her big break came. She was given an entry level position with a large corporation and she met Craig. The world seemed right for her again. For me, too.

The second year, still not easy, was better for both of us. Before that year had passed, Lisa had been promoted to management and had become engaged.

Because of, perhaps in spite of me, Lisa had found her niche at last. Sometimes now when she calls just to see how I'm doing, I know she cares about me as a person. I have one of the bonuses of being middle-aged. My daughter and I have become friends.

9

Habits

Today is wash day. Even when the children are home and I wash all weekend, come Monday morning I find myself digging around in closets and bathrooms looking for at least one load of dirty laundry.

My dryer broke two years ago, but I like hanging clean, fresh clothes in the sun. I like the sweet, sunny smell that soaks into each fiber.

Mrs. Carpenter likes to hang her laundry outside, too. We usually meet at the ditch between our houses and talk. We talk about summer's quick exit, about high utility bills and low Medicare benefits. She is past seventy, her hair snow-white.

I tell her that Lindsay is home from school to have her wisdom teeth removed.

She tells me about her wisdom teeth, and her grandson Larry's.

"Being young's on their side," I tell her.

"Yeah, you're right," she says.

I mention that she needs another permanent.

She scoops her hair back with both hands. "Aw, you ain't got time for that." She laughs. "Besides I'm old. It don't matter."

We agree on next Tuesday.

I reach for my laundry basket. She turns to go back inside.

I watch her walk slowly across the drive. Before she

reaches the door, she stops to rest one hand on her hip. She pushes the other hand through her cropped hair and continues her ritual, staring in thought for a while, then glancing up at the restless clouds.

"I am old," she always reminds herself aloud to me. I wonder. Is she afraid? Is she afraid the way I am sometimes afraid? Does she look at me and wish she could be middle-aged again the way I sometimes look at my daughters and wish I could be young?

She says, "I am old."

I say to Lindsay, "You are young."

I am neither.

10

Tears And Ice Water

My mother didn't seem angry but she snatched a quart jar from the cabinet and went quickly to chip it full of ice from the box in the pantry, then poured water over the chunks of frozen glitter. She seemed to be in an awful hurry as she stepped out onto the back porch, jammed her wide-brimmed gardening hat soundly on her head, and went briskly across the back yard, through the long, wooden, swinging gate into the pasture.

I watched quietly from the doorsteps until she locked the gate behind her, then I ran to follow, calling, "Wait for me! I wanta go too!"

She stopped abruptly and looked back. "No!" she said. She was crying. I didn't ask again. She turned quickly and continued her steady strides up the slight incline to a clump of trees atop the hill.

I slipped my small, sun-browned feet through the bottom rung of the old gate and pulled myself up, resting my chin on the top rail to study her movements more closely. I saw her wipe at the tears with the edges of her wide white collar. She pulled at the back of her sweat-sticky cotton print dress, trying to fan free of summer's suffocating heat.

I wondered why she didn't want me to go along. Lots of times all of us, and sometimes just she and I, had picnics there on the big flat rock that hugged the hill like a century-old tombstone. I wondered why she cried.

I had seen her cry before . . . a long time before when we

lived in the old house and winter had the whole world frozen up and still. The wind had been blowing fiercely that night, and tree limbs outside my window scraped and groaned against the house when I thought I heard Mama cry.

I pulled my legs free of the heavy covers, slipped down the hallway and stood just outside the half-opened door to her bedroom. My feet stung cold against the icy floor, and I squatted to step on the tail of my warm flannel gown.

I could see Mama standing beside the hearth. Her raven-black hair hung loose to her hips and her white gown was full and long. My father put another log on the fire while Becky hurriedly made their bed. But Mama just stared into the flames, tears glistening on her transparent skin drawn over high cheek bones.

Although I knew crying meant sadness or pain, somehow her tears seemed unimportant to me. She was just so beautiful standing there, her gold ring shimmering in the firelight, her face pensive and unsmiling. I thought she was even more beautiful than the Madonna on the wooden-handled fans at the church.

Then Becky spotted me. "What ya doin' outta bed, chile?" she scolded. "Don't ya know ya gon' freeze?"

Mama turned and motioned for me to come to her. She hugged me tightly and kissed me. I felt her tears on my face and I wanted to stay with her—stay in her warmth and her smell through the cold of the night. But Becky took me back to my bed, and early in the morning I heard our new baby's cry.

Oh gosh! I thought that day as I clung to the swaggering old gate, *Reckon she's gonna have another baby?* No. That's been a long time ago. Besides, since the last one came, I had heard her tell Becky there'd be no more children. There were seven of us already.

I watched her sit Indian-fashion on the flat rock, unpin her hair, and shake it tumbling loose. Then several times she poured some of the ice water into her hands and splashed it against her face. After a while she pushed her long hair back, sweeping it tightly into a neat new ball atop her head.

I meant to ask her why she was crying that day, but, like so many other times, her plight soon lost my interest. Other things, perhaps a wandering turtle or frog, drew me from my station of concern.

For two weeks it had been ninety-nine degrees in Georgia. On Tuesday our air conditioning had gone out. Lindsay and Marcus staged a ridiculous argument over the rightful ownership of a bottle of shampoo, which Lindsay said she had paid for with her very own money. George had left for work all out of sorts. And Lisa called to say her car broke down on the freeway, and there was nothing I could do. Somewhere in the middle of all of this, the air conditioning man called to say it would be two more days before he could get the parts.

We didn't even own a fan.

I brushed at my tears, grabbed the tall glass of ice water Lindsay had set out for herself, and headed for the shade of the woods. I sat on a large pine log to sip the icy liquid and shake the loose tee shirt from my sweaty bosom.

I seemed to see myself that day through the eyes of the child I had been—the barefoot, carefree child who swung on the gate at the bottom of the hill and watched and wondered. I could see my mother—in me—how much like her I had grown to be.

TEARS AND ICE WATER

But I wore jeans and sneakers. I don't even own a cotton print dress with a wide white collar. And the tingling ice in my glass wasn't chipped from a block of crystal in the pantry but easily scooped from a box in the refrigerator that somehow tumbles out plenty for the taking.

My hair was short and curly, but my legs were long like hers and my own cheekbones shone with tears.

I poured some of the water into my hand and slapped it onto my face. No doubt we children had been driving her mad that day too. *And Daddy could be a bear sometimes, huffy and pouting and angry. I bet she felt helpless, the same way I do. Maybe lonely.*

Know what, Mama? All these years I've thought you were in such control of your life. I measured all of my failures by that. Maybe I'm finding comfort today in knowing that you had these kinds of days too.

I leaned back against the stub of a tree trunk and swallowed down the last refreshing drop of water. I stared at the cold empty glass cradled in my hands.

Oh, Mama, how sweet it would be if you could come sit for a while with me. Share stories about quarreling kids, grumpy husbands, smothering heat.

We'd laugh about it, I know, then thank the Lord for ice water and cool hiding places in the woods.

11

Bumper Cars

The children's transition to adulthood seemed to run parallel to my own into middle age, and one seemed no more difficult or painful than the other. All of us seemed too absorbed in our own transitions to understand the struggle or pain of the others.

Little did I realize how many learning seasons I would stumble into, wade through, and stagger out of during this misunderstood age in the middle. Perhaps the most confusing were the seasons of my children. Those cuddly, trusting little creatures who had filled me up with love turned into arrogant, brilliant, voracious behemoths, draining me with frustrations and helpless anger.

When they began the final stage of growing away from me, I experienced panic, freedom, loneliness, pride, and failure. Such a turmoil of feelings sometimes overwhelmed me.

Since the first day I became a mother, I had felt responsible for everything that happened to my children. No matter what kind of problem arose, I felt I must solve it. If anything went wrong, I examined myself first for the cause. If the children experienced disappointments, I was also hurt deeply.

My children and I seemed to be traveling down the same road, side by side, each in our own vehicles. They were on their way to maturity, taking on more and more responsibilities. All the way I kept crossing the yellow line, bumping into them, shouting to them from the window of my old Packard to slow down, to drive with caution, to read the signs. I blocked their slick new roadsters, not willing to give up all my responsibilities. The sensible thing would have been to keep the road open, letting each one pass in his or her own time. But because we didn't realize what was happening, we clashed, preventing any kind of progress.

When they did get into trouble and had to pull over, I jumped out to give them all the assistance they neither needed nor wanted. I was the one who needed to be needed—for a couple of reasons. One was to keep up my image of the good mother, for as long as I was mothering them I wouldn't be getting older. The other was that I thought the time had come when I would be rewarded for supplying their needs.

As far as the "good mother" image went, I thought my role was every woman's role. Lots of times I wanted to talk to Mama about my feelings—about how I really hated having to be everything to everybody. But I had never heard her complain, and I didn't want to disappoint her with the fact that I was weak and hurting and confused.

I wanted to be strong the way Mama had been strong.

If I gave up my strong mother image, who would I be? Just old and weak and unnecessary me.

As a matter of fact, now in middle age I not only felt weak, I felt abandoned. I shouted from my racing old four-door that I was glad they were gone, and I was excited with my new freedom. But in truth I didn't want to travel that road at all—my growing-older road. I unconsciously set up the road block, detaining the children. Perhaps holding on to them would delay my own journey.

It was during this traffic jam that I realized my attitude toward the children was changing. I didn't understand and I didn't like what was happening, but I seemed unable to hold my feelings in check.

Little things played havoc with me. If Marcus or Lindsay rushed in from school with a shirt or tennis shoes that simply had to be washed that very minute, I stopped whatever I was doing, no matter how important, and washed. But it made me angry.

Then if Lisa or Laura needed something special at school but waited late to tell me, I became extremely upset.

Such little things. There was a time when I was thrilled to do things for them, loving them, anxious to let them know they could depend on me. Now I could see myself, the perfect martyr, doing everything for everybody and feeling bitter about it. All of a sudden I decided that for all my work and worry, teaching and tears, I was now due praise and appreciation—shouts of "Bravo!" and roses tossed at my feet. What a bummer!

Even though I believed I deserved certain returns from the energy and time I invested in my children, they went right on living their own lives, while I burned out! Burn-out, I'm told, comes in any task when the promised rewards don't match up. I began to murmur against my fate. *Even when I get tired and depressed, so what? What difference does it make to the kids if I wash their tennis shoes or not? What have I accomplished? They'll just be dirty again tomorrow. The girls will need something again next month.*

The feeling of being unappreciated left my work with no meaning. Then those feelings caused guilt and I began looking for the causes—and some solutions. It had never been easy for me to stay out of God's way with the kids, always going to the rescue, solving the problems, healing the wounds. But that was the primary cause of the pile-up on the little, narrow road we were traveling. Somehow I finally saw that I had to back up and let them work themselves free—let God work in their lives—that our road maps led in different directions, and He knew about both routes.

And once we passed the illfated collision—once our traffic had been unsnarled and time and distance separated us a little, the rewards which I had thought were non-existent began to come.

One Sunday night, after Lindsay had gone back to school, I was particularly irritated. I had warned her that the shower door in the downstairs bathroom leaked, and asked her to check it after each use. But she'd left the carpet soaking wet. Her bedroom, so quiet without her, was strewn with last season's clothes she'd discarded.

I grumbled as I stuffed them back into their boxes and George removed the wet carpet. The whole house, and my life, seemed in pointless disarray.

That night when I started to bed I found a note on my pillow under the bedspread.

> I can't give you any reason for writing this, except to tell you how much I love you. I may not express it well, but just remember I'll always be around if you ever need me.
> Lindsay

Me need her? And she willing to meet that need? How delightful!

The tender letter reminded me of a poem Lisa had written to me after she got out of school.

SEASON OF THE CARNIVAL

*Please don't think I'm unaware
Of things you do because you care.
But what I really want to say
Is thanks to you and "your" way.
I'm glad you are my mom, Mom.*

I didn't think she was aware of my struggles, of my need to instruct her, how much I cared. Her poem warmed me.

A few years later I was sitting at home, missing George and all the kids, feeling isolated and alone, when the doorbell rang. I found a young man standing there with a beautiful arrangement of fresh flowers. I assured him he was at the wrong address, that the girls were all gone and who? Yes, that's my name. Oh.

The note said, *I love you, Mother. Marcus.*

There was no special reason for the bouquet. My son—my perpetual tennis player—lived in Texas now and was just thinking about me. He also wrote me warm letters of love and appreciation.

Laura had almost driven me insane with her ninth grade love affair and her growing determination to marry James. With their slipping around when we insisted that she date other boys, and the constant fear they would elope, I had aged considerably. But I insisted that they wait until her junior year in college. And after the honeymoon, she confided, "I'm really glad it worked out this way, Mother."

Now as I look back down the death-defying, sometimes clownish road which we all have traveled during our season of discontent, I see the little detours as just delays to plan a better way. The washed-out bridges—and there were many—were major rebuilding decisions. Best of all, I found myself looking for the Lord's directions in this painful and happy journey.

PART 2

*Stuck On The
Merry-Go-Round*

12

The Pain

George has just come in from work. I try to tell him something. Later I can't, for the life of me, remember what it was. In the bedroom he takes off his coat and tie and sits in a chair to remove his shoes.

Well, I know right away he isn't listening. I can tell when he isn't listening. My voice rises.

George doesn't like it when my voice rises.

Then he does what he knows I hate—what makes my blood boil! He looks at his lap, shakes his head slowly, and raises his hand like a minister giving his blessing. "Just lower your voice, please," he says. His voice is infuriatingly soft, the kind of soft that reduces my status from *wife* to *child*—or *criminal*.

"Don't do that!" I scream. "Don't you dare shake your head and lift that hand! I'm trying to tell you something important!"

He drops the other shoe and smiles—not a normal smile, but the kind that says to me, "Yeah, I gotcha again. Just settle down now and be a good girl and Daddy'll listen."

Oh, I am furious!

He stands, his shoes in one hand. I grab one of the shoes and before he reaches the closet I draw back and let it go. But just as I do, he catches my action out of the corner of his eye and throws up his left arm.

A bolt of lightning shoots up my arm. The shoe misses him, crashing into the wall.

I grab my wrist and scream through clenched teeth about

his never being willing to listen to me. He throws up his hands as if to surrender and laughs. Not wanting him to know how badly I'm hurting, I run to the bathroom, find an old ace bandage, and wrap my hand and arm.

The pain is unbelievable. Something surely has been broken inside my wrist. Worse, I'm still angry and I feel so foolish.

I sit across the table from him eating dinner. He asks why my arm is wrapped in a bandage. What can I say? "I hurt it when I threw the shoe. Guess that'll learn me, huh?"

George smiles and looks down at his plate.

For five weeks I wear the ace bandage. My right wrist hurts when I lift a plate or type or try to open a door. Finally, on the Fourth of July, I go to the hospital emergency room.

The doctor looks at the X-rays and shakes his head. "Weird. Weird X-rays," he says. "Strangest break I ever saw."

"It's broken?"

"Yes. The navicular bone in the wrist. But I don't know why it looks so strange."

I sit on the examining table and watch him puzzle over my X-rays with the emergency room crew. Finally I confess it's been five weeks.

"Great day in the morning!" the doctor bellows. "No wonder I couldn't figure out why it looks that way."

He walks over to me, holding the X-ray in my face. "You could have come by my office any day. Why did you let it hurt you so long?"

He draws back, hooks his thumbs in his belt, and demands, "How'd it happen?"

No use withholding any more information.

THE PAIN

"I threw a shoe at my husband."

The doctor stares. "I don't believe that," he says. "This kind of break has to come from a fall. It takes a lot of pressure to break that little bone down in the wrist."

"But that's the truth."

He splints my arm and tells me to come to his office later. There he calls his three associates in, one at a time. "Look at that X-ray," he says, then steps back. "Now tell me how you think she did it."

"A fall," each one says.

"Nope," he says quietly, shaking his bald head. "Threw a shoe at her husband."

Each one in turn seems to look at me with disdain. "Is that true?"

"Yes."

"Did you hit him?"

"Missed."

They laugh. After a while it's like a party. Everybody in the office comes in to laugh.

And everywhere I go, for eleven weeks, it's the same—a great joke at my expense.

Although George is being unusually kind about it all, my observation has been that that's the way it is with anger. It boomerangs.

13

Flight

All my life I had heard snatches of delicate conversations about "the change": the unrelenting hot flashes, outbursts of anger, and even madness that came to women during middle age. But it wasn't until I got there that I remotely understood.

What happened came so gradually that I didn't even recognize its arrival until it had settled in for the long stay. My strong self-control began to falter. I felt uptight, on edge. Just about everything made me cry. When I tried to rationalize my feelings, to label things (This is happening because ...), I couldn't make sense of it or get myself any more together. Soon I realized that in my case, as I think is true in many others, menopause had little to do with my restlessness.

George was on the road two weeks of every month, and I couldn't seem to handle responsibility the way I'd done in earlier years. Lisa and Laura were away in college. The financial burden of keeping them there haunted me daily, as I stretched and stretched the dollars for tuition and books and clothes. Marcus kept me listening for another accident. And Lindsay seemed like the forgotten child, with all my concern and energy going elsewhere. Sometimes I cried about that too—about being so worried with other things and other children I missed the joy of sweet fellowship with my last little girl.

Everything that happened became magnified a hundred times in my mind. Anxiety flushed through me over the slightest trial; even misplacing my checkbook or car keys threw me out of form. My whole life seemed to be caught up in movement, never peace—everybody going in different directions. When I awoke in the morning I was either apprehensive about what would happen that day or still unsettled about some little things that had happened the day before. Sometimes our house, our lives, seemed all cut apart and scattered like an animated jigsaw puzzle; yet we all scrambled around in the box, trying to get pieced together in some kind of order.

One night I stood at the sink cleaning cucumbers for dinner. The dishwasher droned in my ears. From Marcus's bedroom loud music vibrated through the whole house. Lindsay screamed, "Cut it down!" George yelled at them both. Just as I thought my head would burst, the cooking rice boiled over.

I threw the wash cloth I held into the sink, grabbed the boiler of rice and ran through the den and out onto the patio, where I slung the pan and its steaming contents sailing through the air into the thick ivy below.

I kept running across the back yard into the woods behind our house. Tree limbs and underbrush clawed at my arms and legs as I ran blindly into the darkness. Finally I stopped and leaned against a huge oak tree to catch my breath. My legs ached as if a long chase had just ended. The bark cut into my back, but I couldn't hear the noise from the house anymore. The voices were gone.

Night air iced cool against my sweaty skin. I let the rhythmic croaks of the tree frogs absorb my thinking. Their familiar song reminded me of home.

Home ... so far away and so long ago. I remembered Mama and Daddy sitting in the porch rockers which they pulled out on the front lawn after a hard day's work. I had lain on the cool green grass and felt dissolved into the vastness of the sky above. I could hear Daddy's voice. "God's sho' been good to us. Earth's warm and rich for another planting. Things'll be good in the store this year."

"And we're all so well, too," Mama added. "Just seems to be no end to God's blessings."

Now the tree frogs' chant rang softer in my ears. I slid down, the bark scratching my skin, and sat leaning against the tree. The sweet murmur of the little creek's rushing water seemed to swell all about me, wrapping me in its song. Tears began to slide down my face. I wanted to go back home, to be a little girl again. I wanted to roll in my soft plush grass and fill my head once more with little girl dreams, innocent and pure ... to bask in the security of Mama's and Daddy's love.

I thought how much I'd like to erase all my life and start over. *I'm just not ready for all this pressure and worry.*

I crumbled dry leaves in my hands. "Where's your God tonight, Mama?" I sobbed into the darkness. "Where are all the blessings you always talked about? He's supposed to be my God too. Remember? But look at me now. I don't feel blessed. I'm drained—spent."

I pulled my knees up close and rested my face in my hands. "I don't want to go back," I whispered. "I wish I never had to go back into that house again."

After the tears dried tight on my face I waited, listening to the night sounds.

"I hate to cook," I suddenly said out loud. "All these years I've been cooking and cooking and they've been eating and eating and they don't even know how much I hate it. And they don't care. They don't notice fresh flowers on the table or pretty napkins or candlelight. Why do I do it?

"Because I'm supposed to, I reckon." I laughed at myself.

FLIGHT

I saw myself at the carnival again, but this time I was the side show, splashing all the gaudy colors of a real, live pity party. I sat perfectly still for a long time—the pain still with me—the confusion and emptiness—until I felt strangely refreshed. Being alone and escaping to the memory of a time without responsibility had let loose a flood of relief. The night air seemed to have soothed away the bitter edges, and I felt amazingly free, separated from the disarray in the house.

As I began walking slowly back to the unfinished meal, I realized that my frantic race into the night had been more than an angry outburst. I had made a discovery. Separating myself physically from my family had been a positive thing—an act of change, and there in the quiet darkness my soul seemed to rest, the burden seemed lighter.

The floodlights at the corner of the house had been turned on. I lifted the blackened boiler from the ivy, feeling a little smug inside.

That night was a beginning of new growth in my life. Finding time to be quiet became a precious freedom, and the search to learn who I really was began.

Starting the climb up to the patio, I glanced back at the woods and felt a sweet kinship with its darkness, its glowworm dance, its treefrog song. It was all mine.

The glass door slid open easily. My family had missed me. They were hungry.

14

Strangers

The time came when rushing from the house in anger or hiding in the woods was not enough. I began to rebel in more dramatic ways to the mold I had been put into—had put myself into. The mold was the perfect wife. No one had told me what my role should be. From observing my own mother and the mothers of my friends, I took the role to be one of nurturing and loving. My mother seemed perfectly content in that role, and I felt that my life would follow the same pattern. For a good many years it was so.

Then came middle age, jolting me from my complacency.

Over the years George had become completely absorbed in his work and I with the home, but along the way we dedicated joint energies into one effort—for the children!

Then one morning I got up to find the house too empty, too quiet. I looked at George across from me at breakfast and silently cried out, "Who in the world is that?"

We suddenly seemed like strangers living in the aftermath of a great performance. The signs were still there, the leavings—empty rooms with ravaged closets and dresser drawers. Souvenirs and old letters, odd belts and trophies abandoned in the dead heat of our children's flight to their Shangri-las.

Now I found myself in a different season, on the back side of the carnival midway. Disquieted, bewildered, I ran about in fear and anger.

STRANGERS

My husband became my unrecognized adversary. A silent war began, but most of the battles were fought inside me. I hurt so badly that I couldn't even look for a safe place to let my wounds heal.

George had traveled for so many years that he'd given me all authority with the children. In so doing he seemed to have melded into the background of our lives. Not being around for Lisa's and Laura's piano recitals, Marc's football games, or Lindsay's school programs seemed to exclude him in many ways which we all regretted. But he had no choice.

When he first went on the road, I'd relate every little detail of our week to him when he got home. But after a years or so that seemed to be something we didn't need to share anymore. Our worlds were beginning to divide: his into travel and work and mine into home and the children.

Now my time with the children had ended, but George still had his work. Perhaps for that reason, I began to resent him. He was holding his world together while mine dissolved. I grew more and more jealous of his work. When we got married I had thought he would complete me, fill my life. Looking back, I think I expected this of him partly so I could stop doing my own inner work of growing up. But instead of clinging to one another, we grew lost in separate worlds, and now mine had come apart. Now I needed someone to help put it back together, to pick up the pieces and put *me* back together. I tried to tell George how I felt, needing to be something to somebody; but he only told me I was foolish to have such fears and longings.

Dominated by anger, I felt I had no control over my life. I felt unsure about everything: my abilities, my worth. Maybe I had been taught by example and by lesson in childhood that I could not be happy without my husband's approval. Or maybe that idea just grew into my thinking through the years. But I had given George and the children the power to validate me, to make me okay. Once the children were gone that power was his alone. I was hungry to be praised, to be lifted up as special in his eyes. I wanted him to tell me that I was still necessary, that he needed me. But I feared that in truth he really didn't need me anymore. His years of traveling had made him quite able to care for his own needs.

So I rattled around in a house too big, with too little to do and with my self-esteem registering below zero.

My thoughts turned again to ways of escape. For weeks at a time I slept like the dying sleep, not willing to face my inevitable end. Then I went on a decorating kick and wallpapered the whole house, losing myself in color and design.

The woods became a more precious haven. I spent whole days there. The library, lined with orderly rows of books and furnished with comfortable chairs, became another hideaway. The gracious librarians never asked me why I came. Quite unaware of my flight, they only welcomed me.

I did my grocery shopping late at night when George was gone. Sometimes I even drove out to the airport to sit among strangers, listening and watching. The scenario eased me and gave me a sense of being anonymous. I could be nobody or pretend to be somebody.

I went for numerous counseling sessions with psychiatrists, psychologists, and marriage counselors, but they had no quick, easy answers. Some of them encouraged me to try to work things out for myself. But I didn't want to work it out alone. I *couldn't* work it out alone.

STRANGERS

I ran away from home more than once. I simply packed up and went to visit friends or family. Sometimes I drove across country by myself, stopping in small towns or cities in search of answers, in search of peace. Once I rented a beach house in Alabama. Running ... running ... always I seemed to be running, because it was too painful to stay.

Physical ailments plagued me. I went from doctor to doctor and hospital to hospital, hoping to find a cause for whatever seemed to be destroying me. But the results were always the same: a cheery good note that I was okay.

But nothing in my world was okay. I felt somehow betrayed by George. Angry that he had let this happen—that I had let this happen—that I was left with no purpose and no one seemed to care. Our private world fell apart. How could we have been so unaware? Why couldn't he fix it? Why couldn't I find an answer?

My first clue about what to do had come when some of the kids were still in high school. One day my friend Kathleen asked me if I would give a program to a ladies' club in another town. I was reluctant although the idea appealed to me. Kathleen knew how insecure and incapable I felt, but she believed in me and boosted my ego by encouraging me to try.

I did.

I wrote a long rambling piece of prose about my childhood and read it after my talk. Everybody there seemed to think I'd been reading my writing for years. They were very impressed.

My self-esteem leaped!

Soon I was receiving invitations from church groups, social and professional clubs. With each appearance I became more confident. I was excited to be moving out into a world that saw me as a vital individual—not the cringing coward I knew myself to be. My depression seemed to stay away for longer periods of time and everything took on brighter colors.

George was home for a couple of weeks a month, then back on the road. But the changes in me seemed to merit his recognition. I always told him about my speaking jaunts, giving all the boring details, and he said he thought it was great. But more and more I began to feel that my attempts to be "somebody" were more of a threat than a reason for approval—especially when I began to receive nice honorariums.

One night I was invited to give a Mother-Daughter program at a large church banquet in Atlanta. The presentation was received with much praise, and as I left, the program chairman handed me an envelope. "A love gift," she said.

I was on a real high when I got home, but George wasn't in a good mood. When I opened the envelope and stared at what seemed to me like a very large sum of money, I handed the check to him. "Can you believe that?" I asked.

He looked at the piece of paper then handed it back. "You spent more than that on your new dress and the drive over there, didn't you?"

His thoughtless remark devastated me.

Later Lindsay called. I had to share the evening with her. I needed somebody's approval.

"What does Daddy think about it?" she asked.

"Not much, I guess. You know how he is."

"Is he okay?"

"Yes. He's okay, I guess. Watching TV," I told her. "He loves that TV."

STRANGERS

She hesitated for a moment. "Mama, he's just not like you. That's all."

Her defense offended me. "What makes you say that? I know he isn't like me."

"I just mean you and Daddy are two different people, you know? I wish y'all weren't so locked up in different worlds all the time."

That was it ... we were locked up in different worlds. I didn't grasp the meaning of being different then. First I needed to learn to be still, to understand who I was, and to like myself better.

15

Middle-Age Miracle

All the desires and hopes of my life prod at me now ... pushing me for a realization or at least a commitment.

Everywhere, all the time, scrambling around in the world of middle age, I felt as if I were searching for something. Something I couldn't call by name, describe, or even remember when I had had it last. Its absence stung as real as a strangling nightmare, then slipped out of reach like a dream quickly forgotten.

If my friends felt this same absence, they never told me. Their discontent seemed to manifest itself in problems with children and spouses. But some nights I lay wide-eyed in bed, my mind whirling for clues to this elusive thing that seemed to grow more formidable every day.

There is no contentment in middle age, I reassured the sane part of my mind. The world has lied to me. Maybe I'll never be content again. I had read about the middle years giving peace and contentment, but they hadn't come to me. There was something missing, and I didn't know what it was or where or even why.

One afternoon when Marcus got in from school, he joined me at the kitchen table. He noticed I had marked up the want ad section of the *Journal* again.

"Looking for another job, Mother?" he asked.

"Maybe."

"What can you do?"

I crumpled the paper and smiled at him. "Make meatloaf and have pretty babies."

"Who pays for that?"

"Nobody. Truth is I'm afraid I will get hired one of these days."

He propped his elbows on the table. "Why don't you go back to school, Mother? You're always saying you wished you had gone. Lots of women your age are at Georgia State."

What a delightful thought! What a perfectly wonderful idea! But more college money?

He read my thoughts. "Take an evening course. Doesn't cost much. Be good for you."

Two weeks later I enrolled for a night class in Creative Writing at Emory University.

The days following were so filled with excitement and preparation I felt like a six-year-old again, ready for first grade. I spent much time deciding what I'd wear, wondering who I'd meet, fantasizing about how smart I would be, or cringing in fear of how dumb I'd be. I hadn't even known it was possible to study writing. Fact is, I always thought that John Steinbeck just got up one morning and wrote *East of Eden*. I knew I had a measure of talent. I'd been writing stories since I got my first round, red Coca-Cola pencil in the little country schoolhouse at Williamsville. But I didn't know someone could help me do it better in a night class. The idea put me on a *real* high. I went about the house with visions of best sellers floating around in my head.

When the first Monday night came, I was giddy. I even reprimanded myself in the bathroom mirror. "Hey, settle down, girl! It's just a simple class. No big deal." But I couldn't stop smiling.

SEASON OF THE CARNIVAL

I drove across the city early to get a feel for the campus before class. When I opened the car door, the crisp, cold air brushed my face refreshingly. It seemed to sieve out thoughts of the disorder I'd left at home: Lindsay's unfinished dress on the sewing machine, the sink full of dinner dishes, and the clothes to be folded. I pulled my coat closer, grabbed my little zippered briefcase, and ran quickly across the street to clear the way for an oncoming car.

As I stepped up on the sidewalk, I felt an unusual bounce in my walk. My feet moved anxiously around the administration building. Beyond, a much longer walk lay stretched across the quadrangle to the building where the class would be held. There, about halfway along the desert stretch, I believe a miracle happened.

I had not intended to stop; I just did. I looked up at the starry sky and inhaled the cool air deeply. I felt a smile on my face as I held my head still heavenward. I kept standing there, trying to identify the feeling. There seemed to be a soft light around me, warming me, caressing me. I felt wrapped in contentment.

All at once I knew what was so wonderful. The part I'd lost, what I had been searching for, was almost within my reach.

It was me!

I had been looking for me!

At that moment I knew that *I* was a real person and tasting the sweet wine of that knowledge. As if God's eyes saw me only, I knew He saw me as an individual. Not George's wife, not the children's mother, but just me, standing there alone on a campus sidewalk. I didn't want to move. Even when another student came along and I finally walked on, the warmth still held me.

Sitting in class, still basking in that feeling of peace, I

heard the instructor call my name. "Ora Graham."

The words sounded familiar, but I didn't answer. If she had said "Mama" or "Honey" or . . .

She looked about the room. "Ora, where are you?"

The feeling couldn't have been more dramatic if a full orchestra had been playing a fanfare for me. My heart was singing as I stood to be recognized, I felt special and new and set apart.

I don't recall much that went on in class the first night. I just sat there marveling in my own feeling of newness, of *being*.

I realized that the carefree young girl I had been when George and I married had not naturally grown into the common-sensed, middle-aged woman I had become. She had instead stopped being, tucking her free spirit neatly, almost reverently behind all the "ought tos" and "shoulds" and "should nots."

Yet serving my husband and nurturing my children had been right. What I had most wanted to do had brought joyful fulfillment to my life.

But now my services were no longer in such demand; I was sandwiched in change. That happy-go-lucky, young girl was stirring free of the place where she had been tucked away, wanting to blossom again, be watered, and have a place in the sun.

The sensation was frightening!

It was wonderful!

16

From The Pages Of ...

Not only did I take night classes and spend time in the woods, I found one place better than all the rest—and it was right at home. I kept a journal there ...

Day 1

The child-me awoke this morning. The child I was so long ago, always in search of hiding places—snug secret dens with cracks or holes or vacant spots from which to peer out at the world.

In an uncluttered corner of our basement, my search has ended. I set up a wobbly black table as a desk, glued together a cracked lamp, and dusted off a worn-out green chair. A threadbare blue carpet covers the cement floor.

I have gathered all my books and manuscripts and writing materials from dresser drawers and cabinets and cardboard boxes. I've cleaned out Mr. George's old filing cabinet and all of my work is now neatly labeled in folders.

I go about my household chores nurturing my secret. I made a pact with myself—the world must never come to this place with me. My little corner is a place only for me, to think about positive things ... to study, to write, to pray.

Tonight I shall sleep with the same mysterious excitement I knew as a child when I found a new place of my own—a place where little sisters couldn't go and big brothers didn't want to.

FROM THE PAGES OF ...

Day 13

In less than two weeks, my cubbyhole study has begun to turn my life around. A place to run to—a place my family doesn't even know about and probably will not care about when they do. So private. So very *mine*.

One window, but it sets high up and I can see only tree tops from my desk.

There are smells of old quilts and moth balls, cement blocks and molded leather. I even like that about it ... smells that for the rest of my life will remind me of this time ... this place ... and this special new feeling my little makeshift hideaway is giving me.

My place—it's been here all along and I never even saw it. But that's my way, to be so caught up in the hunt that I overlook the treasure.

Day 19

Today I got up worried about something. I still do that—worry about something I can't identify—just let it sort of gnaw at me all day long.

But now I've come here to my place and the world is not with me. That's the wonder of this grubby little corner in the basement waiting for me, like a secret lover in a candlelit country inn. Waiting to hold me and quiet my fears and give me peace.

My place is a peaceful place. Quiet. Sometimes I read aloud or sing or just stare at nothing for as long as I like. I fell free and in tune with God.

But something more wonderful than a secret tryst is happening to me here. I'm falling in love with words again.

Day 21

Today I brought George here to my place. I think he

must feel sorry for me, seeing me truly proud of a nook so lacking in comfort and decor. I saw him touch his nose in protest of the musty air. He suggested that I buy a two hundred-watt bulb for my lamp, which I will do.

He smiled at me the way I used to smile at the kids when they could wait no longer to show me their secrets.

He managed to say, "It's nice. Yeah, it's nice and quiet down here."

Today, the new novel. Maybe the Great American one. About a country girl named Sarah. People from the rural South seem always in my mind. Their rich talk, their loving and hating. Country people with their unpretentious wisdom humble me, make me want to share the peace that seems so restful in their faces.

City life! How contrary to my yearnings.

Day 32

A man, who as a boy roamed the woods, fished in the pond, grew tall and strong. His laughter rings in my head. His walk, his hands, his guarded smile—I've memorized them all.

Guyton dear ... your pain has finally ended!

At dawn we gathered, one by one, from faraway places to our father's house in sorrow that such a day had come. We embraced one another, sharing grief, finding comfort in a touch. We came to say good-bye to you, our father's firstborn son.

I feel empty and lonely. I am reminded of my own mortality.

Day 75

Every day I'm writing now. I'm enrolling in a writing class at Mt. Paran next month. It only costs ten bucks. I can cover that from my penny can and returnable coke bottles. Won't that be a story when my Great American hits the market?

My life! Seems so filled with good things lately—things that I love, not just family. Even the family is beginning to seem downright pleasant now.

I believe their attitudes toward me are changing. Or am I the one who's changing? Maybe. I'm having new feelings of hope lately, with less pressure to do everything. Today I left the dishes in the sink until after 3:00 P.M.! And the dirty things just sat huddled there with smeared faces waiting for me. Oh, what a slovenly housekeeper I have become! And oh, how not-guilty I feel!

Day 101

Growing older ... I am growing older. I look into the mirror and see my mother's face. In the faces of my children I see my own. Sometimes I look at George and wish he had been more, then wonder how he's been so much.

I feel greedy, giving, and guilty all at the same time. I envy the youth of my children and long for my mother.

This season of the carnival! Ever with me these days—restless, faceless like the wind, warning me not to fall yet waiting to swallow me up when I do.

I thought time would be a healing thing.

Day 109

This morning from my kitchen window something suddenly tapped my memory bank and out came images of lonely country places and the distant coo of a dove. Fields spread out beside me with rows of bushy green cotton, curving and swerving away and away. I saw mules and plows. Grasshoppers leaped into the dry hot air. My bare feet moved slowly through silky dust along the road ...

Then I snapped out of it. Wanting to go home, thinking of childhood has come to be a sign that the present is too crowded and busy. I spin back to pick up tapes of spacious time and leisure to ease my weary day.

Surgery ... finally it has to be. I am afraid.

Day 146

The writing course is going great! I met a girl named Audrey who says she likes my writing. Today I'm working on an assignment.

Mr. Hirthler said, "I want a statement that you truly believe. Then write a story to prove it."

My statement: Sometimes things happen to us as children that lie dormant for years. Then something trips a memory, and we're able to apply the lesson to our lives.

Now I'm having trouble remembering one such time to write about. My head holds so many colorful memories, one will soon come blurting out, I hope.

Spring will be here soon, with marigolds and daffodils yawning at the sun and honeysuckle hugging the fence, tormenting me with scents of lost childhood. The creek will rave with brilliant greens, maverick bud-faces and brown-eyed wild ones. Stray dogs and Mrs. Carpenter's tired old cat will be creeping through the brush to the cool stream.

Back home, plows will be turning the warm, rested earth for another planting, and everyone will pray for a bountiful harvest. Mama used to tell me how good God was not to bore His children with one long season. I'm glad He was so wise, but my season with her ended too soon.

I miss her in the spring.

FROM THE PAGES OF ...

Day 152

The pact is broken. I cannot keep the world away from my place any longer. It's here with me today. It came last night, this heartache. George! The kids! Rejection! Everywhere, rejection slicing into me like narrow blades of fear, cutting away the good, leaving me empty, and alone.

Paul said in the Bible to count it all a joy—adversity. But I cannot. I can only cry and wonder.

Where is it, Lord? The abundant life You promised. I claimed it for myself. I remember the day, the hour. I wrote it in a book somewhere. Today I need to *feel* it. I need to feel like the child of the King.

If somebody in this house would just hear me! That's all I want: a listening ear and understanding. I have needs, too. Things seemed to be working out again, you know? Like every day was April, easy and patient and full of new promises. But today I'm stooped in hopelessness, shielding against the winds of doubt and bitterness.

I've forced myself to come here today to read Your Word and seek Your face. And sadly, Lord, I've come only after everything else has failed.

If trusting is the answer, help me to trust, for I feel betrayed. If forgiveness is necessary, help me to forgive, for my heart is hostile and angry. If thanks must be given, help me to be thankful, for my lips cannot speak.

If joy is to be found, Lord, help me to find it, for my eyes see only sorrow.

Day 160

Today is for rejoicing! The world looks clearly beautiful when the clouds have shortly passed away. I've been singing all morning, and the dogs howl along with me. They're happy, too. Happy that my tears have stopped, my sorrow all dried up.

I feel so like an autumn leaf caught in the wind sometimes, seeming not to know if I belong on the tree or the ground.

How dear to have a God so willing to forgive my anger and my not trusting Him to work things out with my family or my world. He heard my cry. He always hears my cry.

Today I shall praise Him all day long! Praise Him and thank Him and feel wrapped safely in the purple of my King!

Day 169

The wedding is done.

I heard the processional playing. I wanted to enjoy the moment, but my mind kept scanning the lists at home. Did I forget one last detail?

Suddenly the music softened, and I saw her turn her face to his, declaring her love. But my eyes saw her a child again, running to me across the meadow...arms outstretched, running to me. I wanted to hold her close. Yet I was happy for this little girl who bewitched me with her lilting call, "Oh, Mother, I love you so."

The reception was full of laughter and pictures and good wishes.

"Good-bye," she said, and other things I should have told her filled my head, other things I meant to say.

She kissed her father and when I turned, she had gone.

The wedding was so lovely, but good Lord, I'm tired!

Day 180

I turned in my story assignment last night. I really like the class. So many new people and they all like to write!

FROM THE PAGES OF ...

Marcus taped the session I missed last week. He's such a sweetie! I know he wanted to be frolicking on the tennis court, but he told me he didn't mind since I was in the hospital.

I'm up these days, my sad moods slowly leaving, and I'm regaining a little strength. My life seems to have new meaning now. Writing so fills me, makes me wonder why I ever have down days. Maybe they really were caused by my need for surgery.

Got a dozen new pencils today ... that always helps. I love pencils!

I'm planning to attend a writer's conference at St. Simon's Island in June. Gotta save a lot more pennies or drink a lot more Cokes, one!

George says we can handle it. He wants me to go.

Day 188

Class went great again last night! Mr. Hirthler read my story. He says it's very good. "Miss Jenny's Sunshine," I call it. About a lady I heard pray when I was a little girl and spending the night with her daughter. I like the story, too.

My new friend, Audrey, said "Miss Jenny's Sunshine" sounds like a *Guideposts* story to her.

I don't want to go to bed; I can't sleep anyway. Reading *East of Eden* again. I love that book! George is gone again, but I don't feel so depressed alone.

Day 236

Mailed "Miss Jenny's Sunshine" to the *Guideposts* contest this morning. Crossing my fingers.

George wants me to go with him to Alabama next week. I need to get away. It'll be nice to lie in the sun and rest and eat good food—food I don't have to cook! I'm thinking my next house will not even have a kitchen . . . just serve Saran-wrapped sandwiches and tin-can Tabs from the service station. They don't taste half-bad if you're really hungry.

Day 242

A summer storm rages outside my high-up window. Thunder rolls. Thirsty trees bow and scrape their parched foliage in gratitude, rescued at last from the suffocating heat. I feel so snug here in my place. Today is a good day. George and I are going to the mountains this weekend. I'm excited. Been so long since we ran away from the world together. We don't really know each other anymore. I wonder if he's lonely, too.

Day 253

The dogs and I have spent most of the day at the creek. Orky fell from our walk pole into the water, and I couldn't stop laughing at her. She came scrambling up the bank, spitting and snorting and slinging water from herself. But she got right back on the pole and made it across to the other side.

My dogs teach me things . . . how to keep trying when I fall.

Day 271

I won! I'm going to the *Guideposts* writers workshop! It's been two days and I still cannot believe it. Miss Jenny, I love you!

My first thought was how I wished I could tell Mama. What joy that would bring her. She always encouraged me and her absence is my only touch with sadness today.

I'm thinking about the first stories I wrote as a child in

FROM THE PAGES OF ...

the little country schoolhouse near home. Strangely enough, "Miss Jenny's Sunshine" tells about that little school too. But more than strange—I called to tell my brother Frank. He runs the store back home now that Daddy is gone. He was happy that I won, he said.

"Somebody stopped by the store today asking about you," he told me.

"Who?"

"Margaret Wheat." I couldn't believe what he was saying. Margaret Wheat was the "Iris Cole" in my story. Frank didn't even know what my story was about, so he couldn't know how the coincidence was affecting me.

Margaret and her husband have just moved back to Kosciusko to retire. I have not heard from her since we were sixteen. But the very day I learned I won the *Guideposts* Award with a story about her mother, she appears at my father's old store and asks about me.

Miracles! All around me now.

I'll be going to New York to study with fourteen other winners from all over the United States. Catherine Marshall will be there. Dr. Peale. John and Elizabeth Sherrill and Arthur Gordon.

It boggles my mind!

Day 289

From my New York mountaintop experience back to my place. What a switch! But how dear this corner is to me still, a place to savor all the excitement of my wonderful trip. Even in the beautiful Wainwright House, I remembered my blue carpeted corner, with the green chair and small window. Now both those places have a special charm.

I almost felt like a girl again at *Guideposts* ... so many

interesting people ... such good fellowship.

George is planning to convert an empty bedroom into a study for me. I'm happy and amused. All of a sudden Mother is somebody!

It feels great!

Day 408

My new study is carpeted light green, with green and gray wallpaper. I have a mahogany desk, a credenza, and a super-good chair. There are many bookshelves, and the room is full of light. There is a pretty upstairs view from the double windows. Squirrels play in the trees. The little narrow creek below is a sea of dogwood blooms in spring.

George's effort to settle me in such comfort pleases me, but so far I haven't written much of anything here. I think I miss the smells. Smells and the memories of why my first place was created—a place to search for survival.

This move is another change for me, and like a tired, old bear, I'm reluctant to move out of my warm familiar den to venture into another place.

Although this is clearly a better place, it will take time, as always, for me to accept the good that so often comes with change.

PART 3

Safely Home In Loving Arms

17

Love Messages

It seems to me that the way to show the spirit of God is by loving. But what is the best way to love?

Most of the answers I seek about life these days come to me in the simplest way and always unexpected. My surprise is a combination of delight and dismay.

That's the way it was when my counselor reminded me, as Lindsay had done, that George and I were "simply two different people."

The "different people" flashed back Lindsay's words of more than a year before—her childlike warning that she saw us as two people who had different ways and attitudes.

"Locked up in different worlds," she had said. Now this counselor who has studied human nature, knows all about God's laws and understands personalities, was telling me the same thing. And because he was also young, I decided that in middle age, I should have accrued at least enough objectivity to listen. So I did.

"Different people send out different love messages," he said. "There's a fundamental conflict in being different and learning to live with someone different from ourselves."

Oh, for the wisdom of youth!

I worked at digesting his words and pondered my position. The idea of having to embark on a whole new learning season after all these years did not appeal to me. After all, if we hadn't learned to live together already, the job of trying again seemed like a fruitless chore for me.

But I was tired of our silent war. I needed to rest, and I longed to find a good relationship with George again.

I thought my husband didn't love me because he didn't praise me or declare his approval. Now I was supposed to recognize that his style of loving was different from mine. I decided to accept this challenge. My wait wasn't long. The messages were indeed there.

As I cranked up my car one morning I noticed the gas gauge registered full. I smiled and thought how George always took such good care of my car. Of course! My full tank of gasoline was a love message from him. I thought of other things he did, like helping me clear the table after dinner at night, doing the vacuuming, serving my breakfast in bed sometimes on weekends. Messages everywhere I turned.

During our years together I had not learned to accept George's quiet, easy-going ways as just being different from mine. Just because he never told me I was clever or helpful or pretty didn't mean he thought I was not all of those things.

He was different, all right!

Our love language was so different that we missed each other's signals, leaving both of us empty. I expressed my love with words; his signals were acts of kindness and concern. We were different people with different languages of love, unable to teach each other what the loving messages were. But I was beginning to learn.

Learning to live with someone different isn't easy. I had thought George knew what I needed, but he really didn't. So I had to look realistically at my expectations of what others could do for me. I wasn't being fair to expect him to be everything I wanted him to be. I had even been unfair with myself, trying to be everything to everybody.

Different expectations and different kinds of communication became the key to learning to live with our different selves. Soon I was learning lots of things about my husband and about myself, and about how foolish I had been to depend on my family to make me whole.

I had been blinded to many of George's signals by my silent demands for a certain kind of love message, rather than accepting the only kind he knew how to send. As I learned to recognize, accept, and appreciate his love language, I was able to let go of some of my anger. As my attitude changed toward him, he seemed also to be changing: letting go of his private world.

Although he didn't understand why I should be angry, he knew the fury was real. The change came about so slowly sometimes I wanted to shut up in my own lost world again, but I was eventually able to talk frankly with him about my fear and my bitterness. If he felt my reasons were unwarranted, he told me, and his protests helped some good therapy to evolve. Being able to express my anger—just saying the words, "I have been angry about this because ..." seemed to dissipate the bitterness.

I no longer try to be the perfect wife. And although George's approval is still important to me, I've discovered that I can be happy with my own approval.

Still a long way from being perfected as my Creator has promised I will be, I'm learning a lot about who I am.

18

Finally

We had had some good rains during the spring and early summer, but large oaks shaded our little front yard, and the tons of grass seed we'd planted refused to grow. Even after time, liquid grassgrower, and genuine cow manure, nothing happened. Our only hope was to cover the bald spots with something green.

We decided on ivy, since it was the only green thing I'd ever kept alive for two consecutive seasons. Soon my early mornings were spent planting little sprigs of ivy along the drive, and my shovel and I battled the hard, red Georgia clay with stubborn fury.

One morning my neighbor Barbara ambled out to her mailbox and called to me: "Hi there. I told Bob last night at dinner I was gonna get me one of those hysterectomies. I never saw anybody with so much energy."

"Well, you ought to get one. It's the best thing that ever happened to me," I told her.

"I have a friend upstate who had one, too, and she's as pert as you. That's all she talks about, how good she feels."

"Yeah. I think I'll ask the Mayor to declare a Hysterectomy Day so we can all get together and talk about our operations."

"You better wait til I get mine!" She laughed and walked away.

As I went back to my digging, our words resounded in my head and I giggled right out loud. *How silly! Hysterectomy Day.* I laughed again. As I placed the fragile ivy into

FINALLY

holes in the hard ground, I remembered every single event surrounding my surgery twelve weeks before.

Oh, it was going to be one of those days. A giggle day. I had them often, and I giggled some more, remembering.

The chain of events all started back when the young gynecologist first threw me into this middle-aged state with his gentle, southern respect. The next year I found a nice, middle-aged gynecologist. He also told me I needed a hysterectomy, but he had also told me I was pregnant. So at last I found a middle-aged doctor who spoke my language.

"Well, it's up to you. You're gonna die if you don't."

Still I waited. Two more years passed, and each time I went for my examination I told him how great I felt. I declared to myself that the occasional pain in my lower back was from wallpapering the kitchen with orange and red wallpaper, that the ache penetrating my entire left leg from thigh to toe was from a turned ankle.

"I'm not gonna fight you," the doctor said, "because you'll be calling me soon."

His arrogance had begun to offend me.

"I'll think about it," I insisted, and left his office telling myself, "Maybe in five years or so."

But as the weeks went by, the pain in my back got lower and the ache in my legs got worse and, like an old-timey record player winding down, I slowly stopped ... just after I made it to the couch.

For ten weeks I lay there, getting up only for food intake and output. I groaned when I got up ... sighed long and pitifully when I lay back down. Whoever happened to be in the house heard how awful I felt as I described my pain in minute detail. Nobody stayed home much.

I wanted to cry all the time, and most of the time I did.

Finally George exploded. "I've had it! You've got to go get something done!"

At long last, I found a really neat, soft-spoken, middle-aged doctor who simply told me *I* had made the right decision.

We set the date for my hysterectomy in three weeks. I was truly afraid. Millions of women have successful hysterectomies, but I felt I was the exception. Convinced that it was the Good Lord's plan for my exit from this earth, I set out to make preparations for my untimely demise.

I reviewed the weeks I had spent incapacitated and I realized, in a self-justifying way, that I'd been somewhat rude to my family. In fact, in a moment of stark truth, I knew I had become a mean, grouchy, middle-aged whiner.

I became gentle, passive, humble, kind and considerate. The "new me" sickened my children, but George was delighted. He even wanted to postpone the operation, no doubt hoping to spend a few more days with the angel who had come to take my place.

I spent hours writing long, tender letters of farewell to each of my children, who, if the truth were known, had brought this horrendous thing to bear in the first place. For two days I searched for a place to hide my letters so they would be easily found after it was all over.

"What a tragedy it would be," I mumbled as I rummaged for a place in my chest of drawers, "if I hid them too well and the kids never benefited from all my loving advice."

Lindsay was drying her hair when I confided in her about the letters and their whereabouts. I made her promise that they were not to be opened unless and until the end had come.

"I promise, Mama," she said, and never turned off the hair dryer.

FINALLY

Of course, I did not do a farewell, but I did fare well. Great, in fact. My doctor glowed when he examined the fast-healing incision. He "oohed" and "aahed" about how beautiful it was.

Happily, he said that he'd given me an artistic bikini cut. Yes, he had. A scar is never pretty, but one that smiles is really not half bad, depending on the way you look at it. I was impressed that he took such pride in his work. Lucky for me. He could have made the darn thing frown.

Ten days after my reprieve from the jaws of death, I went home to discover that my children had read my tender letters of farewell, and I was humiliated at not having died.

On Monday morning George, having satisfied his loyalty to me by staying in town the entire ten days of my hospitalization, purchased one hundred aspirin tablets in a childproof bottle and eight cans of noodle soup for me. And left town.

I don't even like noodle soup, and I never got the aspirin open. I hurt so badly and no one was there to hear me cry. I cried anyway and prayed, and even thought of suicide. But heck, I'd lost twenty pounds and I decided that this was no time to die.

Imperceptibly, I improved.

Eight weeks from operation day, I walked into the kitchen, became nauseated by that ghastly orange and red wallpaper and decided that was the day to change it.

I went out and bought some bright green and yellow paper. As I lifted my arms high to begin smoothing out the first panel, I stopped, I didn't hurt! I didn't hurt anywhere!

I stretched out like a rabid bat. "Good heavens!" I cried. "I'm healed!"

So on that hot summer morning a few weeks later, as I chiseled at the red clay, hoping to cover the bald spots in my yard with ivy, I kept thinking about that green and yellow wallpaper.

What a change!

19

Already?

*Where are the years that stole my youth,
And made my child a woman?*

I was wiping the cabinet tops with a soft soapy sponge that Saturday morning. Laura was loading the dishwasher while her husband James sat and finished his coffee. They were visiting us, as they occasionally did, for the weekend.

"Those big old trees out there sure are naked," I said. "All this cold rain . . . Daddy says every year we've got to get them cut."

"Mama," Laura said. "I'm going to have a baby."

A knot twisted in my stomach as though she'd hit me, and my ears started popping. All I could do was slip the sponge under the faucet and stare out the window.

"Mother, did you hear me? I'm pregnant."

I glanced around reluctantly. "You sure?"

"Yes, we're sure."

Tears began stinging the edges of my eyes.

"Well, that's *good*, Laura," I managed. "I mean, if both of you are glad."

James sat smiling like the proverbial cat.

"We are, Mama. We're really happy about it. Been five years, you know."

That long? No, it can't be! Seems like just . . .

Then the other children came in and everybody began

laughing and talking, congratulating, teasing George and me about becoming Grandma and Grandpa. I couldn't think of anything wise and wonderful to say like a good mother should.

I knew I ought to toss the sponge aside, hug her close, and tell her I was happy too, but I couldn't. I just kept right on wiping that cabinet top, back and forth, back and forth. I couldn't look at anybody, like an embarrassed first grader who'd forgotten her lines in a school play. As soon as I could leave without seeming obvious, I went quickly down the hall to the bathroom, closed the door, and set my tears free.

That night I lay in bed staring at the dark. I didn't understand how I felt, or why I had to feel confused about such a happy event.

Is it that old "aging" thing come back to play with my mind? Maybe. I don't want it to be that. I don't think I'm still afraid of growing older. Maybe I just hate for Laura's cute little body to swell, clumsy and out of proportion.

I turned to George. "How do you feel?"

"Huh?" He snorted out of sleep. "What'd you say?"

"How do you feel? About the baby, I mean."

"Okay," he mumbled. "I think it's okay."

"Listen, I've got some really strange feelings about it. Wonder why?"

He didn't answer. Asleep already. *That's really neat*, I thought. *George is sleeping so soundly.* How I wished I could be so stable. I lay there (I don't know how long) wondering about things. Worrying. Wishing. Hoping.

Then he stirred from sleep and put an arm around me. "Don't worry, it's okay," he whispered. "She'll be all right. Go to sleep now."

And I did.

ALREADY?

Several weeks later as I was scrounging in K-Mart for a good buy on typing paper, I noticed a little spiral notebook. It had I LOVE U in scrambled letters on the cover, with three adorable little girls, one sliding down the V, one on a stool next to the U, and the littlest and cutest near the bottom. A round glowing sun peeked over the top, with a bear in an apple house. In the lower right corner a perky duck was busy with his brush and easel.

The picture touched my heart. I bought it without really understanding why. Sometime later that day, when my writing was going badly, I studied the picture again. Almost without realizing what I was doing I picked up a pen, opened the notebook, and began writing.

Dear Little Baby,
 I don't really know how I feel about becoming a grandmother. I think of Laura's glow as she talks about you and I'm glad. I see James's pride and I'm proud.
 But how do I really feel? Apprehensive about Laura. Apprehensive about me, older now, seeing time has removed youth from my face. Maybe it frightens me a little. Could be I'll start to live in the past, trying to bring back my youth or trying to bring back the childhood of my own children. Both my grandmothers were very old when I was a little girl and they lived in the past, always telling me how my mom and dad acted when they were little. I enjoyed their stories. They gave continuity to my world.
 So welcome, dear one, and until you're really here with us, I'll fill this book with thoughts about you and prayers for you. I'll even write a story for you about your mom.
Grandmother

I closed the little notebook and held it, admiring again the cuddly babies on its cover. *The letter inside is to a real person*, I thought, *part of me*. He or she is someone I'll know and love, a little child who will no doubt stand here beside my desk, saying the dearest things and thrilling my heart. How marvelous!

By the time our little Erin was two years old, my letters had become more than just love letters from a grandmother. They were my feelings, not only towards her, but about our world and our morals. I would tell her of my prayers for her, that God would give her a teachable spirit, a discerning spirit. Sometimes I'd write her memories of my own childhood dreams and longings.

What if, I asked myself, I'm not around when my grandchildren grow up? What if I'm not here to tell them stories about Grandma Lindsay and Aunt Matt Alford? How will I let them know that I lived in a simpler time but that God's laws don't ever change, no matter how twisted social morals become. What if? What if?

So I began making tapes, telling her, and other grandchildren the future might bring, about growing up in the little Mississippi town. I told her stories about visits to my grandmother's house, of horses and wagons and dinner on the ground and homesickness for Mama. I wanted to tell Erin all the things I'd forgotten to tell her mom. That seemed to be my way, always getting caught up in living and letting little things get by unsaid, or undone, or unprayed.

Eighteen months later, Lisa and Craig announced that they were expecting their first child. I was glad about it. No knots in my stomach this time—no tears burning. I just bought another notebook.

Her name is Afton Leigh. And now Laura and James have another little girl, Allison Ryan.

ALREADY?

I suppose that's the way middle age is, a terrible time of not accepting things, followed by that quiet acceptance.

20

Joy

My granddaughter is with me today. Her name is Erin and her hair is blonde and shiny the way her mother's hair was shiny. We eat oatmeal and drink chocolate milk for breakfast. She dresses herself. She will be three in ten days.

I set up her table and chairs in my study. She unpacks her tea set and places the cups and saucers on the table, along with tiny yellow napkins I made from a leftover scrap.

Rummaging through my dresser drawers I find a soft, satiny slip, and with safety pins, we create a flowing gown for her.

She wants a headband. I fold a bright, sheer scarf.

"I used to make your mommy play gowns when she was a little girl," I tell her.

She smiles.

"I am a queen," she says.

"And a very elegant one, too," I boast.

"Did my mommy be a queen too?"

"Why, yes, I believe she did."

There's much work for me to do, many pages to type. A warm summer rain is falling outside my window, and I watch for a moment. The slick, green ivy below spreads like glass across the yard and down to the narrow creek. I like summer rains, but I roll my paper in the typewriter and begin.

"Ganmurver," she says softly, "you like a cup of coffee?"

JOY

"Yes," I tell her. "Yes, please," but I don't stop typing.

She eases the small cup beside the typewriter, then touches my arm gently with her little hand.

"Ganmurver, you like sugar?"

"Yes," I tell her. "Yes, please." I keep typing.

After the pretend spoon of sugar dissolves, she waits for me to drink.

"M-m-m-m. Very good," I tell her. Now I'm typing again. "Thank you."

She busies herself at the table, not speaking. After a while she pushes quietly between my desk and the credenza and leans her head against the window pane.

"What do you see?" I ask.

"The rain," she says.

"What else?"

"The trees."

"What are you thinking?"

She sighs softly. "I not thinking, Ganmurver. I looking at the rain."

My fingers stop their pounding. I am caught by the beauty of her pensive profile against the glass.

"Do queens like rain?" I ask.

"Yes, ma'am."

"I wish I were a queen," I tell her.

She glances quickly around. "But you can't be a queen. You the Ganmurver."

"Of course." I smile and touch my head. Surely there's a crown there somewhere. How else could I be here in the presence of such a royal princess?

21

Leftovers

Sometimes it seemed that my entire life had been spent being married and mother and master to a variety of pets. The list is too long to remember, but I suffered through the grief of favorite dogs and mindless drivers, cute kittens and macho canines, baby chicks and chicken eaters. Once Marc had a quail named Spiro T, hatched from mail-order eggs in his very own incubator. Spiro T lived only until his fourth day. That was a gloomy day, indeed.

After the kids went away to school, only two little dogs remained in our care. Puppy was a spry eleven-year-old with soft, round eyes that seemed always to beg. Stocky and close to the ground, he had a peculiar little limp in his right hind leg. After every three or four steps, his leg jerked up sharply, as if in pain, then his walk became normal for another few steps. But he could leap five feet into the air to catch a ball. He became the neighborhood canine showoff. For a while he was called The Babe, on account of his ball-playing ability.

When Marcus was gone his little dog became more special to me. Puppy made it seem that a part of my little boy was still around, still performing and begging and needing praise.

Our second leftover was eight-year-old Orky. She had been Laura's dog, a replacement for one that a mindless driver wiped out. When Laura left for school, she gave Orky to Lindsay, and when Lindsay left, Orky became mine. Dainty like the girls, she filled some of the void, prancing excitedly when I clapped my hands.

But she wanted to be like Puppy. She copied the way he barked, the way he slept on his back, and the way he walked. Although she had no deformity, Orky limped on her right hind leg. The dogs became a great item of conversation for our visitors. Everyone seemed struck by Orky's deliberate imitation of Puppy.

I loved my dogs. They were my companions. When I was lonely, they whined against my legs. When I was happy, they barked and danced. When George was out of town, they protected me, climbing watchfully into their own beds at night, then blaring the news of daybreak with barking and gleeful parading about the house, urging me to get up.

Every day we walked through the woods to the creek, Puppy leading the way, Orky hopping behind. In the summer they enjoyed splashing in the cool, clear water of the sand-bottomed creek, and they romped through the fallen leaves of autumn.

A tall oak tree, unable to hold to the bank during a rainy winter, had fallen across the creek. Its roots jutted up on one side and the curve formed at the base of the trunk made a perfect backrest. "My meditation seat," I bragged to friends. A place for remembering and for trying to forget, for asking God and for giving thanks. When the dogs tired of play, they settled at my feet, waiting, still keeping guard.

Puppy died on a rainy Sunday morning in August before his fifteenth birthday. George dug a grave in the woods behind the house. He wept openly as he covered our little friend good-bye.

I grieved much too long and dared not let anyone know

how deeply the loss had affected me. But I still had Orky, and I clung to her. I talked about the flavor of her food at feeding time, asking her which she preferred. I told her how fresh and clean her little bed smelled after a washing, and when I returned from shopping I asked her if she had missed me. She'd dance and squeal and leap at my arms as if a long-awaited reunion were at last realized.

Marcus laughed at me. "Good Lord, Mother. You're talking to the dog as if she's somebody."

"She is. She's my friend." I turned to Orky. "Aren't you, sweetie?"

"Aw, come off it, Mother. You know what I mean. It's not healthy talking to a dog that way."

"Why do you say that?"

"It bothers me, that's all. I don't like to hear you asking her questions as if you expect an answer. You gettin' senile or something?"

Of course I'm not senile! Silly about the dog, yes. Senile, no.

Neither Marucs nor I knew it then, but the dogs and the trips to the woods were helping me work through some of my middle-aged adjustments. Little Orky had become much more than a leftover in my charge. She had helped me find a whole new way of expressing love.

Every day when we made our way down the creek, we paused beside Puppy's grave. Orky respected it, moving carefully around, sniffing at Puppy's favorite tennis ball which George had placed on the mound that day. Then she glanced up at me: *Is the tribute over?* Reassured, she tripped off down the path, her little hind leg still limping.

That's the way people are, I thought. We copy someone else to find their own identity. We all want to be strong. I remembered the girls plopping around in my high-heeled shoes and Marcus making a razor from a stick to play

LEFTOVERS

"Daddy." Everybody copying somebody, wanting to be like the best, the wise, the strong.

As Orky hopped down the creek, I wondered if my children could be crippled by copying something in my life. They thought I was strong.

On another rainy Sunday almost two years after Puppy died, when Orky had grown old and sick, she disappeared. She had never left the house alone before, not even to go to the creek. I went through the stormy woods calling, crying, and hoping my sweet little pup would find her way back home.

She never did.

I seldom go to the creek anymore, but when I do, my head overflows with memories of my little friends.

"You know, Lord," I cried one day, "I can't even count all the dogs that have come and gone from our house over the years. But Orky was so special. I still look for her when I drive down the street, still think I hear her excited squeal.

"I want her back, you know? The way I want my children back when the winter rains come, want them back inside my house, warm and snug in my arms."

Is it wrong to love a little dog so much? I wondered. The way I loved Orky?

I think not, an answer seemed to whisper.

"I'm glad."

It's just part of letting go, you see.

Oh. I've tried to do that: let the children go . . . and the dogs.

But letting go means you must change.

I don't like change.

I know. Change is painful, but if you want to grow . . .

Grow? Me, Lord? I'm growing old.

Not old. Up.
But I miss the kids, the dogs, the good times.
Why do you struggle so? Why not rest, let change make you strong?
But I am so weak, Lord.
Then follow Me.
The leaves rustled.
The wind touched my face.

22

Father's Day Dog

It's hard to clear the air and blow off steam at the same time.

The trouble started brewing on a Mother's Day. This one was no different from any of the others. I knew there would be no gifts from my family; however, cards of love and good wishes did come on Saturday from two of the four children.

On the actual day of Mothers, Laura and James brought seven-month-old Erin for us to keep while they spent the day at Lake Lanier. I couldn't help enjoying the baby. But I was uneasy because she had a fever and was cranky.

Dark came and her parents had not returned. None of the others—Lisa and Craig, Lindsay or Marcus—had called or come to visit. George had given me a sweetheart card and served my breakfast in bed that morning. Intellectually I knew that he couldn't know how much I wanted a gift unless I told him, and I never did. I suppose I thought he should have known by himself. Finally I voiced my feelings, and of course, they came out as a complaint.

Then I confessed to him how hurt I was because the children didn't give me a gift either.

He was defensive of the kids. "They never have given you a gift on Mother's Day."

That opened my ire gate.

"I know that very well. But I had always hoped that

when they got out of school and had money of their own they would be more thoughtful."

"Well," he said. "I sure wouldn't let that upset me."

"Wouldn't you?" My voice rose. "Well, it has upset me! And another thing . . . all my life since the kids were little I have secretly hoped every Mother's Day that you would send me a corsage."

He gaped. "Huh?"

"Yes, and I always got you a Father's Day gift, no matter if it was small. Last year, remember? I got that beautiful plant for your office. Remember?"

He took little Erin from me. By now she was crying pitifully, her response no doubt brought on by my tone of voice. I followed him to the kitchen. "And you remember about your folks and mine. We always gave them—"

"Yes," he snapped. "Of course I remember."

"And those kids of ours will spend more money on beer and pretzels than a gift would have cost."

He agreed, but I needed a person to lash out at, so I got back to the corsage story. "Yeah," I said wiping my tears back, "I always sat in church on Mother's Day, envious of all my friends smiling like saints with their corsages. That really hurt me, you know?"

He wanted to apologize. "I didn't know," he said softly. "You never told me."

"Oh!" I squealed. "If I gotta tell you . . ."

And I knew at once how silly I was to want my husband to know already what I'd never said before.

Later, when I stopped crying, George agreed the children had been thoughtless. They hadn't been all that generous on Father's Day either.

By the time Laura and James got back that night, Lisa,

FATHER'S DAY DOG

Craig, and Lindsay were there, too, to eat. Marcus never showed up.

After they wished me a "happy happy" and left, I cleaned the kitchen. Helping me, George completely sided with me about "my" day. He vowed that we would go away every Mother's Day from then on. And he would buy me a gift, too.

Neither of us, however, said anything to the kids about it.

On Monday I did receive Mother's Day cards from the other two children.

A month later, on Father's Day, Laura and James bounded into the house like Santa Claus. They carried a big box which held an adorable little blond cocker spaniel, a Father's Day gift for George.

My insides began to churn. The veins in my neck swelled. I thought my whole head would simply blow off like a popped cork.

How dare you! I wanted to shout. *Haven't you been listening to me at all? I don't want another dog! I won't have another dog!*

George held the little puppy as if a precious child had been placed in his arms, adoring the newcomer and smiling. I felt like a heel. I hated my anger about the new responsibility, but I had learned that I could not pretend it wasn't there.

Then George looked at me and he knew. I could see that he knew, but what could he do? Caught in the middle, he knew I didn't want a dog and he knew why. But there he sat, holding his Father's Day gift (an expensive one, too), knowing if he kept it I'd be angry and if he didn't they would be hurt.

He said nothing.

Finally I began to cry. "I really don't want another dog," I said.

"It's Daddy's dog, Mother," Laura said defensively. "From all of us."

"But Daddy's not here two weeks in a month. Who'll take care of it? I've told you kids for years that when Puppy and Orky were gone we would never have another dog. If your daddy was going to be here all the time, it would be different."

Laura began to cry too. "I don't think you love Daddy anymore, Mother," she sobbed.

"That's not fair, Laura!" My voice was rising.

"I can't believe you, Mother. It's not like you to be so selfish."

"Now wait a minute," I shouted. "Orky's been gone less than a month. I'm still looking for her."

"That's why we thought you'd—"

"You didn't think of me when you bought the dog. Listen to me, honey. I've been feeding dogs and cats and kids for more than twenty-five years. I'm tired of it now. Don't you see?"

"No, I don't see," she choked out. "I don't understand you. We bought this dog especially for Daddy."

I protested. "But now I can go places when Daddy's out of town without having to hurry home to feed the dog. I can even go with him and not have to worry about a kennel or somebody to look after it. Don't you understand that?"

"I just can't believe you! This doesn't even sound like you, Mother!"

She flounced downstairs. Everyone else sat in silence. I guess they couldn't believe me either.

After a while I followed Laura. Calmer now, my eyes

burning with dried-up tears, I tried to talk more softly. "I might as well tell you how I really feel, Laura. It hurts me when you kids don't buy me a Mother's Day gift or even a birthday gift, for that matter."

Surprise registered on her face. "Is that it, Mother?"

"No," I said. "I'm pleased that at least you got your father a gift for Father's Day, and I know he's caught in the middle. But we've all talked about never having another dog, and you just took it for granted that I didn't mean it—that I'd still be here to take care of it."

I marveled at what was happening. It was the very first time in my entire married life that I had been able to say, out loud, for the whole family to hear, how I really felt. And I was saying it quietly.

But when they left, things were still not resolved. The puppy stayed.

I told George how jealous I was that they were so generous with him and had forgotten me. He agreed I should be. But then I said, "Why didn't you just tell them that this is my house—that if I don't want a dog, then that's the way it has to be?"

He looked puzzled for a moment, then he said, "You know, you're right. I should have done that, but I just didn't know what to say. I really didn't, and I'm sorry I didn't."

He told me he would take care of the dog. I wouldn't even look at its sweet puppy face for fear my heart would change. The little thing howled all night in the garage. George kept getting up to see about it.

For the next few days George was in a quandary because on Monday he had to leave town for a two-week trip and I'd planned to go to Kosciusko. Part of the time during the week the puppy was with us I felt ashamed for acting the way I did. Why shouldn't I be willing to care for the dog? After all, it was a little thing, and no doubt I'd fall in love with it soon, if I ever looked squarely in those big soft eyes. But another part of me stayed unwilling to be locked into a situation I hadn't asked for and had in fact broadcast against. In simple truth, I was tired—tired of being the keeper, the nurturer. I even resented my children for being so thoughtless. I wanted to keep my new-found freedom.

Laura and James came on Sunday, and I told Laura that we wouldn't be there to care for the dog. She offered to take the puppy, telling George to call her when he got home.

They never brought it back.

I was so sorry for my show of anger, because I knew Laura and James had acted in love to buy the dog. And I knew they really thought the puppy would be a good healer for me since losing Orky. Their gesture was not a direct affront to my wishes.

Most of the time anger distorts reason and leaves scars, but some of the time honest anger vividly exposes needs and creates a close bond.

A year later on my birthday, George gave me a great surprise birthday celebration and all the children came home. We had dinner out, a birthday cake, and happy birthday songs. Their gifts were stunning, and I felt so good to receive them. I had no feelings that they were acting out of duty. I watched their faces as I unwrapped each gift, their childlike expressions, waiting anxiously to see if I liked their choice. Their love was genuine and so were my happy tears.

Isn't that just like God to turn a really miserable situation into a joyful celebration?

23

Qualified?

> Wanted: Young, experienced, bright, personable, mature woman.

My appointment is set for two o'clock. The time is one-thirty and I'm lost.

On this dreary autumn day, clouds press against my car window and wind whips misty rain all around as I drive up and down Jacob's Ferry Road. I'm looking for Benson Street, so I slow down at every corner, trying to read the street sign. Finally I stop the car to read my directions again.

"Benson Street does not dead-end at Jacob's Ferry Road," I speak back to the sheet of directions, then slam it to the floorboard of the car.

Just ahead I spy a telephone. I'll call!

But the wind outside is strong, and my new permanent will frizzle out like Little Orphan Annie's! I'm about to cry but remember my makeup. I pull up beside the telephone booth and debate my situation.

Today, my makeup must not smear and my hair must not frizzle. Everything must be perfect for my job interview—my first interview since I became middle-aged. But inside I resent having to go to work. I resent being forced to work by family economics. Perhaps that's why I feel everything must be right—so my ire won't show.

But so far nothing has come off in order. I can still smell

the burning motor in my washing machine and see the tub of wet, soapy clothes to be dealt with when I get back home.

My pantyhose are too short—doggone long legs—and the heel on my left shoe is just ready to pop off. I am frightened and my stomach will not stop quivering.

Finally I decide I have no choice. I must call.

"You're not too far away," she says. "Benson Street dead-ends on Jones Ferry Road."

I could have sworn she told me Jacob's Ferry Road.

When I finally locate the address, I am stunned at the plushness of the office. My mind is doing quick flashbacks to the crowded little office where I once worked, the busy street smells that drifted in through open doors and windows with the sounds of car horns and squeaking brakes.

But here soft music fills my head. The reception area has Oriental rugs, with rich, polished mahogany furniture and live plants everywhere. There are two matching love seats and a French Provincial coffee table centered with a luscious arrangement of silk flowers. Copies of the *New Yorker* and *Smithsonian* lie like advertisements beside the brass compote holding pale yellow mints.

Suddenly I remember my glasses—resting on top of the smoking washer. The realization of no magnifying power for my aging eyes hits me in the stomach—pow—right in the quivering, and I feel sick. I must have my glasses! But it's too late now. I glance down to see which handbag I have. The black one. I sigh relief, remembering I have an old pair in the side pocket. One of the lenses is cracked but I can at least read with them.

The receptionist is away from her desk. I wait for what seems like a very long time before I take a seat on one of the couches. Presently, a beautiful young woman comes in

QUALIFIED?

the door, waits, then sits on the other couch. I decide she is also an applicant.

Elegantly, she stretches for a magazine. I reach for one, too, and no sooner get it to my lap than I remember about the glasses. Not willing for anyone to see the old cracked pair, I simply open the magazine and gaze at the blur and squint my eyes trying to see the large cartoon at the bottom. The effort makes me dizzy.

When the receptionist returns I place the magazine back on the table and move across to her desk as gracefully as I can. She looks up, pitifully young.

I tell her my name. She smiles and hands me an application clipped to a board and asks me to complete it. Even before I get back to the couch, I'm panicking. There's no way to avoid getting out the old cracked glasses now.

I turn away from the young woman and scramble in my handbag for them. Even the case is frayed and seedy looking. I slip my spectacles free and ease the case back inside the bag.

I stare at the fragmented print on the page. The diagonal break in the left lens pushes half the page up about two inches and none of the sentences meet. I keep shifting my head around, trying to make sense of the questions before I realize all I have to do is close my left eye. One-eyed now, I stare some more.

My name and address and telephone number I fill in without any trouble. My social security number is here somewhere among my credit cards and stuff. I juggle through it before realizing my driver's license number is the same.

The "past experience" space stops me dead! I want to look up and ponder a bit but I remember how silly the little, round, metal-rimmed glasses look—so out-of-style—so I keep my head down.

I have no degree, my experience is over twenty-five years old, and I understand that nobody uses pen and ink bookkeeping anymore. I list it anyway. Writing the date is painful—I probably worked before the receptionist was even born.

Now I find a whole list of skills to check. Calculator. Billing machine. Teletype. Typewriter. I check that. Speed. 60 wpm—I'm guessing. Mag I. Mag II. Payroll. On and on the list goes, and my checking is limited to bookkeeping and general office skills—which are outdated skills at that.

This is a responsible position I'm applying for, and my civic endeavors and community projects over the last quarter century seem like such insignificant undertakings I'm ashamed to list them. I feel so insecure, so incapable. I wish I were at home working on the washer.

I complete the form and take it back to the young girl at the desk. She rises and motions to me. I misunderstand her and head for a moment to the wrong side of her desk. Seeing her lead the way down the hall, I stumble back after her, my loose heel making me wobble on the deeply carpeted floor.

"This way?" I ask.

She doesn't look back but answers me with a "Yes, ma'am" that is so distinctly southern "respect-for-my-elders" that I wish I had a cane to support my trembling legs and protect my teetering heel.

The personnel director is not a day over twenty-five. She stands and shakes my hand when I enter, then asks me to be seated. My heart is booming like wild drums. *No wonder*

QUALIFIED?

middle-aged women can't get back into the work force, I think. *Their daughters have all the jobs.*

"We've had tremendous response for this position," she says softly. "Seventy-five calls, thirty-five of which are qualified."

My ears start popping. I hold my hands tightly. I can feel my face flush. I feel so old and clumsy, and I'm angry at my humility. The mother in me wants to speak bluntly to this young girl: "I can do anything, do you hear! I am able to do this job."

But I don't. I know she is much smarter than I and much more in tune with the business world. She'll know right away I'm not the one. I realize I'm competing in a world so foreign to me that I want to cry. I ache to run away and hide and never expose my incapable self again.

I stumble through the interview somehow, hoping I haven't sounded too dumb by trying to sound too wise. She tells me that five applicants will be chosen to come for a second interview, at which time the department head will discuss actual duties in detail.

"I want the job," I tell her. "I enjoyed meeting you. Please consider me."

Back in the car, sweating profusely, the tears swell up in my eyes and my leg won't stop jerking on the brake. I can't wait to get home. I'm anxious to get my hands on those soapy clothes. I can do that easily—wring them and rinse them and hang them on the line. I'm good at things like that. *What is a Mag II?* I wonder.

Three days later the personnel director calls. I've been selected as one of the five to come back. I'm bowled over! Excited! Happy! Scared to death to face another interview! But I agree to be there on Monday at two o'clock.

Now I'm getting in the big league, the top five out of

thirty-five. *Not bad*, I tell myself. George tells me that, too. I'm feeling more confident now. It's been a wonderful dose of pep for my ego. I have to have a new dress, my hair cut, and nails done. My glasses I'll put squarely where I cannot forget them. But ... I'm not really sure I want to go to work. In fact, part of me is still angry. *Why should I have to go to work at all?* I push those feelings aside.

For some unknown reason (most likely prayer) nothing goes wrong on Monday—that is, nothing major like a burning washer or too-short pantyhose. I am prepared.

For two hours Mr. Whitlock and two of his assistants brief me and quiz me about the job. The position is so interesting, the office so lovely with a view of a hillside. The two young women with whom I'd be working are certainly pleasant. I try very hard to impress them all.

Back in my car again, I feel a gnawing pang of discontent. I can handle the job, yet murmurings stir inside me as if warning me that I am about to commit myself to a second career. *A real commitment is a long-term thing*, say the voices. Day in and day out I will be coming to this office. No more casual walks in the woods when I feel the need. No more days of my own. This will be a full-time job and will fill up all of my time.

My body shudders. I crank up the car and remind myself that surely I won't get the job anyway.

Mr. Whitlock promised to call me on Wednesday, if they wanted me to fill the position. By the time the call comes, I have become a complete coward. I don't want the job, and I don't even want to tell him so. In desperation I ask Lindsay to tell him that I want my name taken out of consideration.

Ashamed, I determine not to answer another want ad.

QUALIFIED?

Instead, I head for a temporary agency to find something I can live with ... a short-term commitment I can handle.

24

Family

Today I have come home, to Mama's house.

This big old house that once stood proud and erect seems tired now, stooped with time, settled with age. All the family is here, fifty-one of us—in-laws, grandchildren, great grandchildren. We've gathered from Texas to Tennessee in a chorus of greetings and laughter and hugs and kisses. We're talking, smiling, listening, crying. There're just seven of Mama's eight children left now.

We complain about the heat and wonder how we managed to survive without air conditioning. We survey the land, comment about where the old garden grew, the smokehouse, the corn cribs, and the chicken houses.

We brag about our children and talk about middle age, the thoughtless young, the dependent old. We give each other remedies for wrinkled skin, dull hair, and irregularity. We play the piano and sing with its brassy notes. We tell stories about fear, gladness, and sorrow. We reminisce about Guyton, the brother who is gone now. We lovingly quote our parents and wonder at their patience and wisdom.

We hold the new grandchildren, trying to make the babies laugh, and we're glad they're not our own. We welcome neighbors who drop by. They tell us we haven't changed. We smile and glance at one another, amazed at their wit.

I feel a wild current racing among us as we each see a moment, a day, a lifetime, and know it again. Each of us finds a place apart where we can pause and stare and remember.

Roaming about the grounds up to the old barn, I see it is almost collapsed, its hinges rusty, the weeds grown tall. No longer does it smell of feed and manure and sweaty saddles. There are no signs of me; no proof I was a carefree child here.

The old pump is gone. Only a grassy mound remains. The trees have grown taller, too, and thicker; but none have lost their place in my memory. The hillside is clearly the same, and it is good to feel the earth beneath my feet—this place where I played and dreamed and grew.

I am crying now, in tune with the sweetness of youth and kin and home. Middle age is not too old to remember the young life, to touch and taste and hear and smell. But I let my sensations slip quickly away, the feelings too soft and precious to hold inside.

Today has been a good day.

25

Voices From The Past

Sometimes I see it in a rose
Or feel it in the wind ...
The sweetness of their innocence.

George and I speed down Interstate 75 toward Florida for a week's vacation. Our luxury car seems to float as I nestle back into the velour upholstery and relax in air-conditioned comfort. *Clair de Lune* fills the car in FM stereo sound.

We have looked forward to this, and we talk of our retirement years not far ahead of us. We declare we'll take at least two trips like this each year.

I look at the scenery: white clouds on blue sky, trees and fields so green. I'm at peace.

Just ahead I see a station wagon, overflowing with children. Yesterday, or maybe centuries ago, we sped down this same highway with our children. Yes, I remember. Our station wagon ... hot wind blowing in and out the windows, blistering our skin, rattling the paper bags, tangling our hair. Behind my seat squatted a large box of staple groceries I'd packed. I'd been frugal for weeks to ease the contents out of our food budget. Behind the box were balloon floats, bathing suits, four children, and the dog.

Oh, the picture comes back so vividly, with all that sound!

VOICES FROM THE PAST

Daddy, it's my turn to sit by the window. Daddy, tell Marc it's my turn by the window.

Move over, Marcus. Let Lisa sit there awhile.

Mother, make Marc take Puppy's head out of the window.

He needs to breathe same as you. How'd you like not to breathe?

Daddy, Laura stepped on a loaf of bread!

Honey, you didn't bring bread? We can buy bread in Florida, you know.

No, we can't. Not day-old bread.

Mother, Lindsay dropped her bottle and got dirt on it.

Hand it to me.

Daddy, Puppy's eating the bread!

Good Lord!

Mother, why'd you turn off the radio? That was the Beatles.

Daddy, Marc threw one of Lindsay's shoes out of the window.

Tattletale! Tattletale!

Good Heavens! Her new shoes. Stop the car! How far back?

'Bout a mile.

What does a five-year-old know about miles? We'll forget it.

No! They're new!

Surely you don't think we'd find it now.

Let's go back and try.

Forget the shoe!

How can I? Lindsay's only shoes!

FORGET THE SHOE!

Mother, I got to go to the bathroom.

Honey, let's stop at a service station.

Can't she wait? We'll be there soon.

Can you wait, Laura?

SEASON OF THE CARNIVAL

No, ma'am. I'll try.
Please try, okay?
Daddy, Puppy threw up on Lisa's bathing suit.
Stop the car!
The whole thing, Mama. Puppy ate the whole thing.
Every year this happens! That dog's not coming again!

I still hear the monotone clet, clet, clet of the tires as they cross the seams in the road. I feel the whirl and switch of the breathtaking wind in my face as we speed ahead.

But that's not real. Now I'm comfortable, the heat and wind only a memory. George smiles at me. Did he hear the voices, I wonder? No. He'd be redfaced from the smothering wind and his smoldering frustration. We weren't really living it again. I shake myself back to the present.

Hours later we drive into a lovely motel where we have beachside reservations. George leaves the motor running to keep me cool while he goes in for the key. So different from the way it used to be.

Daddy, there's a nice motel.
They don't have kitchens.
Get one with a pool, Daddy. You promised a pool.
Gotta have a kitchen too.
Daddy, Lisa poked a hole in my float!
Shut up, Marc! I'll patch it!
There's one with kitchens!
Looks crummy to me.
You want the Hilton?
Want one that's clean.
Mother, Laura's eating a banana. Can I have one?
Laura, leave the food alone!
I'm hungry.

VOICES FROM THE PAST

Great day! What a bunch of kids! Every year!
The kids are hungry. We need to feed them.
Okay, okay, let me find a motel first!
Don't get mad.
Who's mad?
You sure sound mad!
I'm gonna get mad if you keep saying that!
Daddy, there's where we stayed last year.
No vacancies.
You never make a reservation!
Never slept on the beach, did you?
Might tonight.
Daddy, I gotta go to the bathroom!
Okay, Laura.
In a hurry, Daddy!
Okay.
She wet her pants!
True to form.
Don't cry, Laura. It's okay.
There's one. There's a motel, Daddy!
Looks nice. Can we afford it?
No, but we'll take it. Hide the dog 'til I get registered. Cost three dollars over our budget. That takes care of our one meal out.
Okay with me. The kids don't mind.
Daddy, where's my patch?
I'll get it! Shut up that crying!
The baby's hungry.
Well, what d'ya think? Is this okay?
This is fine. It's clean.
Where are the children?
In the pool.
Already?

SEASON OF THE CARNIVAL

Now at our luxury motel it is quiet and peaceful. Dressed for dinner we walk past the swimming pool filled with children. I glance at them and the voices come back.

Mother! Mother! Look at me!
Don't go so deep.
Daddy, look at me!
George, Laura shouldn't dive from the high board.
Oh, let her. She's a good swimmer.
Lisa is a sissy. Lisa is a sissy.
Stop that talk, Marcus!
She is, Daddy. Won't get in over her head.
Good Lord! Get the dog!
He's in the pool?
Let him stay, Daddy! Let him stay! He likes it, Daddy.
Can't do it.
Please, Laura, don't dive from there again. Scares me.
It's my float!
It's mine!
No, it's mine!
Take Lindsay. I'll get in with them.
You kids settle down. Don't wet your mother's hair.
I'm watching, Marcus. Yes, Laura, Mother's watching.

Our week is over. The time has been a second honeymoon. We've rested, taken in a little sun, and walked along the beach hand in hand. We've eaten fresh seafood and agreed that retirement would be beautiful.

We head back home. I glance behind me and imagine the dog and all the children, sleeping ... they fill the station wagon along with sand, and floats, and more sand. The kids' sunburned faces shine in repose.

I readjust the belt on my velour seat, brush imaginary sand from my silk blouse, and lean back in comfort.

VOICES FROM THE PAST

The mother in me cries for a time in life that's past, but the middle-aged woman in me sighs. *Ah, sweet bliss. The children have grown up at last!*

26

Love Room

If we do not live by bread alone, how come I'm always standing here among the bread crumb leavings, dirty dishes, and ovens that grow crusty black?

"A middle-aged kitchen?" George echoed my statement with a question. "Who ever heard of such a thing?"

I sat beside him as he hurriedly ate his late breakfast.

"What else can I call it?" I asked, glancing around the room. "Looks great, doesn't it? At last, the perfect wallpaper, perfect curtains, even color-coordinated lustrous new tile on the floor. When else but in middle age could I be so orderly?"

"Always looked okay to me," he mumbled, then gulped the last swallow of coffee. He grabbed his briefcase, kissed me on the ear, and said good-bye.

After he drove away, I lingered at the table, admiring the room I'd labored over for so many weeks.

My kitchen *was* middle-aged. Not chronologically, for the house was twenty years younger than I, but it rested the way I'd learned to rest. The sounds of children were gone; there were no crumbs on the floor. Maybe the absence of those very things, the sounds and disorder, rushed a feeling of melancholy about me.

So much of my life had been spent in kitchens. I reached into the desk drawer and took out my calculator.

LOVE ROOM

On a note pad, I recorded the number of hours I'd actually lived in the room that had hosted so many happy, hectic times.

During my 9,855 days of marriage, I'd spent 28,638 hours in the kitchen. Even after I'd deducted 900 hours for vacations I never took and 60 hours for birthing all four children.

I had washed dishes 20,973 times! I looked at my crinkled hands. How boring! The numbers were staggering, but somehow I couldn't remember it as mundane and boring.

Unhurried by my days as they had now become, I glanced again at the beauty of my kitchen and jogged my memory of the first kitchen I had known.

Mama's kitchen! Of course, in the old house with the sagging back porch. I remembered every inch of that room: the missing pull on the flour bin, the tiny windows, the brown, blistered wall behind the wood stove.

I recalled a cold winter's night as a child, growing up in the little Williamsville community where my father had a general store. After the heavy wooden locks were pushed shut and he'd called it a day, he would enclose my small hand in his to stuff it deep into his coat pocket for the quarter-mile walk home. He seemed unaware of the frantic trot of my small legs as I tried to keep pace with his long, comfortable strides.

Before we reached the long drive to our new house, off the county road, we could see the smoke trailing up high above the trees. Slender shoots of light from the windows lighted paths into the woods. As we made the turn, Daddy's pace quickened. "Bet Mama's cooking ham and biscuits," he'd say.

Closer now, we could hear laughter, and when the back

door opened, the warmth and aroma of Mama's kitchen filled our heads. It was good to be home. Daddy shook welcoming kids off his back as he tried to tell Mama how good the ham smelled, "all the way to the road."

We sat on long, squatting benches, and Mama served golden brown biscuits from heavy iron skillets. The home-cured ham was sliced thick, with red-eye gravy and rice. A feast, it was! But most of all it was a feast of love.

And many a time I crouched in the pantry, my heart beating fast, as I watched Mama pile high a plate of food for a passing tramp.

On the night before my wedding, I found her there alone. She couldn't sleep either. She made hot chocolate, and we talked quietly. I saw in her a softness I'd never seen before. She wanted to tell me things, to ease my fears and heighten my joy. As I stood to go, she took my hand and I wiped the tears from her face.

What a kitchen to house such tenderness! A place to welcome strangers and say farewell to its own.

I poured myself another cup of coffee and thought of the first little house of my own. Young and happy, I seemed to be always busy in the kitchen, cooking, feeding the children, waxing the bright floor, or defrosting the antique Frigidaire.

And daily, neighbors dropped by to borrow an egg or pay back a cup of sugar. We swapped recipes and discussed our children's ailments or mischief. There on my little kitchen table I folded into my sheets and towels the sweet smell of sunshine before storing them away.

And when the last dish was washed and put away at night, I glanced back with pride, at my clean little love room, before I flipped off the light.

Another kitchen, the prettiest one I'd ever had, was

LOVE ROOM

filled with children too, some of whom I didn't even know.

Musical sounds of the Beatles moved right in with me and hung over my sink. I found myself washing dishes with a rhythmic beat. Wet bathing suits seemed to come alive, popping up in little knolls all over the floor as the children stepped free of them when my back was turned.

The refrigerator door kept opening and closing all day long. Peanut butter stuck everywhere, on forks, knives, the dog, the floor. But no one seemed to know that I was there. They handed me things or asked for things as they passed through, but no one heard me call, "Come back and pick up your shoes!"

And there was another kitchen when my mother came to visit. We spent hours over breakfast, after the kids got off to school, talking and catching up on all the relatives.

She made new curtains, a new tablecloth, and rearranged pictures on the wall. She also bought me a new tea strainer, an egg spatula, and a dozen sturdy drinking glasses (mine were jelly empties).

She bragged about my frugal ways, then cooked extravagant dishes. She made cookies for the children and let them create their own design with the dough. Our kitchen was so filled with warmth and love that part of me left with her each year when it was time for her to go.

And in that same kitchen a voice on the telephone told me that Mama had died.

So ... numb and lonely, I finished my coffee. I carefully brushed the kids' crumbs from the table cloth she had made and pondered the impossibility of living without her.

Now I sit alone in my beautiful, middle-aged kitchen. My memories have almost made me cry.

Suddenly the doorbell rings! As I open the door I hear giggling. "Surprise, Mother!"

The children have come home!

In the kitchen, as they help me clear our breakfast dishes from the table, Marcus picks up my note pad and studies it for a moment.

"Gee, Mother, you mean you've spent 28,638 hours in the kitchen? What a work record!"

What a record indeed, I silently boast. But work? Yes ... there was that, too.

27

Frugality

I need to go shopping. The summer sun just won't let up, it seems.

K-Mart always has good buys on spray bottles. I need one to mist my plants.

Yes, there's a pretty one. Delicate little flowers around the bottom. But $2.99? My goodness, I paid only $1.79 for the old one that won't spray anymore.

But this one sure is pretty. Lightweight. I like the beige and brown colors. And it's larger than the old one too.

Still, $2.99 is a lot to pay for a bottle just to mist a few sickly plants every morning. I laugh. Some mornings I don't even remember to do it.

I ponder that.

Peachtree Salvage Store probably has a cheaper one.

So what if it's damaged. It'll still serve the purpose. I'll just walk down the block to see.

No, we don't have any.

I think about it some more.

Maybe A & P.

Yes, I think I saw some there with their plants last week. It's only a few blocks away.

I'm burning up in the car. I wish I had worn a sundress.

I can't believe it! $3.99!

The Dollar Store's next door.

Yeah, we have 'em sometimes. Not today.

I stand under the awning to ponder again.

SEASON OF THE CARNIVAL

Well, I guess I ought to go back to K-Mart. That one is pretty, and cheaper than the one at A & P.

If it doesn't hurry and rain everything will parch.

Maybe I'll just drive out to Kroger first. Not but a few miles out there.

Good heavens! $3.99 too! Ridiculous!

This is the hottest car I ever saw.

With my luck the darn thing'll be gone by the time I get back to K-Mart.

Thank goodness! It's still here.

I'm glad I got this one. Fills so easily. Pretty too.

I'm tired. Rest just a minute.

Guess I'll spray my plants now. Feels good in my hand. Yes, I got the best buy, didn't I?

Who knows? Food Giant might have them.

There are some things about me that even middle age can't change!

28

The Dreamer

Dreams and reality: one is always in search of the other.

When I was a little girl my father scolded me because I dreamed too much. But Mama encouraged me to dream. She said it was good to dream and plan for the future.

Sometimes I dreamed of being a princess or a poet or a waitress in Mr. Mac's cafe. Even more, I dreamed of being a nurse who wore a silver watch like Miss Iva Summerhill. She stood tall and smelled so clean, her nurse's snow-white cap crowning her dark curly hair.

But my overriding fantasy took shape around my baby doll, Lucy. I cuddled her and hushed her cries with promises that soon her father would be home. I dreamed that one day I'd be somebody with a husband and children who loved me.

My dream came true! George and I had been married only eighteen months when our first little girl, Lisa, was born. For a time I felt lost in the real world of motherhood, with diapers and formula and midnight feedings. And trying to order my time was a major problem.

Nevertheless, two years later came Laura, and two more years brought Marcus. I no longer had time even to set priorities. When Marcus was three, another little girl completed our family. We named her Lindsay.

SEASON OF THE CARNIVAL

I remember once when my unmarried sister visited me in all my garish array of sick children in a messy house.

"Gee, Sis," she lamented. "How do you know who you are in all of this? I'd feel so unloved."

Of course, I had no identity problem . . . with four kids screaming "Mama" all day long. And how could I feel unloved with a husband coming home at night giving me passionate kisses while my hands were still busy in a sink of dirty dishes, one toddler tugging at my skirt, another crying from the bedroom, and a hungry cat weaving gracefully against my legs. My Lord! Everybody loved me!

As the children grew, I became submerged in their lives. Then I had to learn that it would not always be so. Lisa's first day of school arrived. I cried. At the same time I realized that she was meant to grow away from me. Soon I accepted that she spent her days at school.

Then Laura's first day came. She left me, her ponytail dancing like spun gold down her back. I cried again.

Marcus's turn came next. Exuberant about his new tennis shoes and extremely pleased about his stiff new jeans, he still looked to me like a little boy lost when I left him that morning.

I cried all day long.

But it was hardest of all to say good-bye to Lindsay. That was the worst one for me. My empty house forced me to recognize that the little private world with my babies had ended.

I found myself spending idle mornings shopping. One day in a variety store, I noticed a mother and her little boy in the back aisle arguing about which sun hat to buy for him. I envied her, thinking how lucky she was to have a child still at home.

As I neared them, the little boy turned toward me. An

THE DREAMER

ache caught in my heart when I saw he was much too old for first grade. His slanted eyes smiled happily as he lifted a chubby, uncreased little hand and mumbled some kind of greeting. Realizing why he wasn't in school, I was too ashamed to look at his mother, not wanting her to feel my pity.

I thought of my children. I had felt their leaving was a tragedy. How ungrateful I'd been to God for their normal development. They were meant to leave me.

I was glad they hadn't grown up all at once, but every year, come September, I grieved. I relished the summer we'd shared, knowing that each season gone spent a part of their youth as the world beckoned them from childhood.

Once they were in school, however, I enjoyed my quiet kitchen until the last one left for college. That day I comforted myself with memories of my own youth—the day I left home.

I remembered the excitement, the anticipation of going out on my own at last. Real freedom seemed to be within my reach, and I was happy.

Yet as I packed I felt the little-girl sadness of giving up my room, my bed, and the view outside my window. The smell of honeysuckle whispered in my head that day as I searched my dresser drawers for little, private things ... my diary, my turquoise ring, and the little locket without a chain I'd saved since I was nine. I paused for a final glance back, and the soft, quiet wallpaper, which had been far too prim for my taste, seemed suddenly bright and pleasing to my eyes. I saw Mama watching me go and I brushed aside my tears when I said good-bye.

But once I'd gone, I stored away my childish dreams and ventured happily into a whole new world. I experienced pleasures I never imagined and sorrows I somehow found the strength to bear. The years were a time of growing, of learning new and good things about myself. And my leaving gave me insight into my mother's gentle spirit and my father's quiet kind of love.

So, when Lindsay left, I was lonely, but I thought of all the pleasure yet to be hers. She would grow and experience the wonderful sense of being new and individual.

Sometimes I wander aimlessly through my empty house, wishing all the sounds of youth would fill it once again. On the lazy Sunday when the children all come home, George and I soak up their vitality, enjoying their music and laughter and entertaining conversations.

And in the evening, when the house is still once more, we smile at one another, sharing pride in our children.

It's true, my best little-girl dream has come and gone. Now I'm going back to rediscover some of the ones which somehow got crowded out. And dream new dreams for the years yet to come.

Epilogue

Recalling the day the young doctor sentenced me to middle age makes me realize just how much I have changed. Much of the change has been painful, due in part to my stubborn resistance. Although there's still a lot of work ahead for the perfecting job my Creator has begun, I'm reaping some of the benefits already.

While I still care about my appearance and work very hard to delay the aging process, I'm no longer in frantic search for the fountain of youth. I relinquished that task, partly because I'm tired, partly because I've learned there is no such thing.

Freedom . . . at last I'm enjoying it. Quite often I bundle up my pencils and paper and typewriter and go with George on the road. While he works I hole up in a motel and read or write or go shopping. In the afternoon when he gets back, we look for museums or simply drive through the city or the countryside. Then we eat good food for dinner without the slightest worry about kids or dogs at home to be fed.

Sometimes when I'm shopping and suddenly realize it's

SEASON OF THE CARNIVAL

3:00 P.M., I stop in the store and think: I don't have to hurry home—not for Little League, not for Girl Scouts, not for nothin'!

It's wonderful!

Yet I still have no trouble at all cranking up my old imaginary Packard with its bright new headlights to chase after the kids, still yelling from my car window for them to slow down and to drive with care—warning that a bridge might be out! But I'm careful not to cross over into their lanes. Sometimes they shake their fists and shout for me to stay out of their way, but most of the time they just smile and wave me on by.

I don't flee into the night from my kitchen anymore, crying and filled with anger. I don't try to solve everybody's problems or load up my heart with their burdens. I really like who I am, and I'm almost never lonely.

Some days it seems as if I'm going home from the carnival, the exit in full view up ahead. I still hear the music, but it's less brassy, even pleasant sometimes. And since the crowds have cleared, I don't feel so closed in. I still smell the smells and see the lights, but I am going home—and with lots of good winnings.

I have finally let go of the merry-go-round and found the everlasting arms of my Heavenly Father—the One I trusted so long ago when I had no idea how that trust would be tested.

I feel so safe and good about this time in my life—the same way I felt as a child that day at the country fair when Mama finally found me and took hold of my hand.

ABOUT THE AUTHOR

A free-lance writer and mother of four, Ora Lindsay Graham describes herself as "an ordinary middle-aged woman who hates being ordinary." Graham has received a scholarship to the Guideposts Writers Workshop and the Southeastern Writers Association award for non-fiction. She lives in Austell, Georgia.